THE COTTON GIRL ORPHAN & THE STOLEN MAN

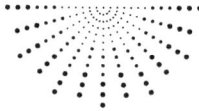

ROSIE SWAN

PUREREAD.COM

CONTENTS

PART I

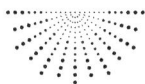

PROLOGUE

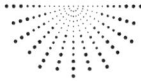

1 **857 - Potter's Cove Vicarage, Bristol, England**

"My love, did you think I would just let you sail away without coming to bid you God speed?" Anne Lockhart nee Cotton held the hand of the one man who had come to mean so much to her.

"My darling," Ernest Lockhart took the hand of his bride of a few hours, "I thought we said our goodbyes outside the chapel. And it's not as if I am sailing away into the New World. We're just going a few miles offshore to rescue our fellow fishermen. Nothing to worry about," he raised both hands to his lips and kissed them, his eyes promising delights to come.

Tears filled the twenty-year-old woman's soft baby blue eyes as she looked at the dark- haired man. His grey eyes seemed to shimmer in the evening light. The sun would soon be gone, and so would he, something very unexpected for a groom on his wedding day.

"When I woke up this morning, it was the happiest day of my life," she said, letting the tears roll down her cheeks. "But now I'm really afraid."

"Don't cry, and most of all, do not be afraid," Ernest whispered, "This is just a routine rescue. I'll soon be home, and then we shall never be parted again, my beautiful Anne," he wiped the tears away, but more took their place. With a deep groan, he gathered her into his arms and put his lips on hers. Apart from the chaste kiss he had placed on her lips a few hours ago when the vicar pronounced them husband and wife, Ernest had never held Anne in his arms.

This kiss was different, and Anne felt it deep in her heart. It held the promise of good things to come, and it also told of a parting that was regrettable. She held onto her husband like she never wanted to let him g,o but the sudden blast of the foghorn made them spring apart.

"That's me," Ernest said, "Keep the candle burning for me, my darling." He kissed her once more, a swift touch of lips, and then he turned to walk away.

"Please come back to me," Anne whispered, one hand over her heart and the other touching her lips. As she watched Ernest walk away until he was swallowed by the dusk, she wished he would turn around so she could get one more glimpse of his handsome face. But he didn't, and with a sigh, she turned and made her way up the rugged path and to the small cottage to await her beloved's return.

And as she lit a candle, placing it close to the window so he would see it when he returned, her lips murmured an earnest prayer for the safety of her husband.

∽

"It's a baby boy," the tired midwife announced, wiping the sweat off her brow. "This was a very difficult birth, and it is a wonder that mother and child are alive at all," she told the tall thin woman standing beside the bed. "I haven't lost a patient in fifteen years,

4

and you can be sure that I wasn't going to let your sister and her baby die."

"Her husband is waiting outside," Marie Winchester said, drawing closer to the bassinet where the little baby lay. "He looks nothing like his father," she commented snidely and the midwife gave her an odd look. That was a very strange thing for her patient's sister to say, but she didn't comment, because it wasn't her place to do so. The snide comment implied impropriety, but the midwife shook her head.

Ruby Setter's work here was done, and whether or not the little baby boy looked like his father wasn't her problem. Having been a midwife for over twenty years, nothing under the sun shocked her. Why, she had once delivered a pair of twins; one of them was as fair as his parents while the other one was dark tanned. Life was mysterious, and as someone who saw the bringing forth of new life on a daily basis, anything could happen. Her concern was the wellbeing of the mothers and babies she delivered, not their personal lives. No one would pay her for poking her nose into matters that didn't concern her. That was why she was well beloved as the midwife of this seaside village, both by the wealthy and the baseborn. Ruby could keep secrets and never revealed what wasn't hers to reveal.

After gathering her tools of trade, which was comprised of a number of small sharp knives, a roll of thread, and some dried herbs, she put them all back in her small satchel.

"I have left some herbs to be boiled. Let the new mother take a cup in the morning and another in the evening. It will help with lactation and also to stop any excessive bleeding," she told the tall woman, who was barely paying her any attention. With a disinterested shrug, she tossed the satchel over her left shoulder. "I'll be leaving now." She paused to see if the woman would say anything. When she didn't, the midwife opened the door, and the first person she saw was the husband of the woman who had just given birth.

"It's a boy, Sir."

"Thank you," he took her hands and pressed a small purse of coins into it. "Thank you very much," and without another word, he rushed into his wife's bed chamber.

1

THE STRANGE CHILD

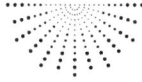

1 *860 – Potter's Cove Vicarage, Bristol, England*

It was one of those dismally warm summer days, and Trudy Foster wiped her brow. This was the second difficult birth she had attended to in a matter of weeks, and she paused as she waited for the last contractions that would see the birth of a new life into the world.

"Mrs. Cotton, just one final push, and your little one will be here," Trudy said, gently rubbing the young woman's swollen abdomen.

"Get this thing out of me now," Jill Cotton hissed, clutching at the ropes that bound her to the narrow cot. Trudy had her own ways of dealing with especially troublesome first-time mothers. They were often as excited and spirited as new mares, and a number had ended up killing their babies. Like any other responsible midwife, Trudy took no chances with her patients. Hence the ropes that bound hands and feet, putting the mother in a spread-eagled position. This particular woman had been one of her most difficult patients, and Trudy was glad that it was nearly all over.

"Here we go," Trudy urged, and shortly the cry of an infant filled the room. "You have a beautiful baby girl." The baby fell silent, and it was a disturbing quietness that unnerved the new mother.

"Why isn't she crying," the mother raised her upper body, resting on both elbows, "Why is my baby silent?" Any mother knew that silence wasn't good when it came to a new-born baby. "Trudy?"

Trudy was lost for a moment, gazing into the deep blue eyes of the little baby she had just delivered. The child didn't blink, and the midwife felt something like a shiver going through her. This was a strange child indeed and had it been the middle-ages, would have been called a witch.

But Trudy wasn't frightened of the child. It was more a case of wonder. In the little baby's eyes, she saw something so deep, it was as though she were looking into the eyes of an old man or woman who had seen many mysteries in the other world and had carried them to the present one.

"What manner of child are you? "Trudy murmured. "What manner of child will you grow up to be?"

"Trudy!"

The baby chose that moment to open her small mouth and let out another howl, and she kicked her small limbs vigorously as if she was angry at having been disturbed from her nine-month cocoon. "Is she all right?"

"You heard her," Trudy chuckled as she did the needful, cleaning up the infant and placing her on her mother's bare belly. "She looks really hungry." Trudy loosened the bonds that held the mother to the bed. Immediately Jill flexed her wrists and reached for her baby.

"She must be very hungry, for I wasn't able to eat anything for a whole day and a half," the young woman received her baby and kissed her forehead. "You are so beautiful," she whispered.

"Go ahead and nurse her," Trudy paused from cleaning the room. "She seems to know what to do."

"Thank you."

"You're a strong young woman, and I hope I will be here again next year to deliver another one."

The woman snorted, giving Trudy a cold look, "It will never happen again. One painful experience is enough for me, thank you very much," her lips tightened. "My body isn't made for such torture, and now that my husband's desire for a child has been assuaged, it is never happening to me again."

Trudy wanted to laugh and tell the new mother that she'd heard many of her patients saying the same thing upon delivering their babies. But a few months later, she would be called back to deliver yet another baby. But the look in this particular woman's eyes made her hesitate, "Do you have a name for the child?" She asked instead.

The young woman nodded, "Salome Victoria Cotton," the new mother announced proudly, "My little Sally."

"Good name for one who will grow up to be very wise and discerning," Trudy said remembering the look she had shared with the child.

"You're very kind to say that. My husband will bring money for your payment when he returns from the coal mines. Thank you very much for your service."

"I believe I can leave you to nurse your baby as I get rid of these. But I'll be back shortly to give you something to help with more milk production and to stop any excessive bleeding."

"Thank you so much."

"Please forgive me for taking drastic measures earlier on and restraining you with ropes. But you were really nervous and if I hadn't done that, we might have lost this beautiful baby."

Jill Cotton gave the midwife a sheepish grin, "I'm sorry that I gave you so much trouble."

"You're a first-time mother, and it was to be expected. Still, I've dealt with women worse than you, some of them even in their fifth or sixth pregnancies."

And as Trudy went on about her midwifery experiences, Jill shut her out, gazing in rapturous wonder at the baby in her arms. After five years of waiting, sometimes tearfully, their bundle of joy was finally here, and she couldn't wait to share her with her husband. Miles worked at the coal mines and, much as he wanted to be around, he had to make money. Jill sighed as she looked around the small cottage that she called home. It had only two rooms and would have been sufficient for the three of them, but her sister-in-law had come to live with them a few months ago.

Jill's lips tightened. She didn't like her sister-in-law and wished the woman would find another place to live, but Miles would have none of that.

"Anne is my sister, and she is bereaved. The poor thing is in mourning, and what better place to be than with her family?"

"She can't mourn for a man forever and besides, it's not like they were even really married."

"It doesn't matter that Ernest was killed on their wedding day. Anne is a widow and she needs as much time as possible to deal with the tragedy that befell her."

"It's been nearly a year. Don't you think she should have found another man by now?"

Miles had glared at her and refused to respond. Jill wanted Anne gone from her house. Now that her baby was here, it shouldn't be hard to make her husband see that Anne's help was no longer required.

There was a soft knock at the door.

"Come in," Trudy called out. The door opened and Jill's lips tightened when she saw who it was.

"I brought some light broth as you requested, Mrs. Trudy," Anne Lockhart nee Cotton said, hovering in the doorway with the tray.

"Get in, child, and place the tray on the table. Your sister-in-law has been delivered of a beautiful baby girl."

"Oh," Anne placed the tray on the table and cautiously approached the bed. A hissing sound had her take a hasty step back. Anne loved her sister-in-law, but the woman was difficult to understand. In days gone by, they had been friends, but after Ernest had died, things between them had changed. What made matters worse was when Miles, her older brother had insisted on Anne coming to live with them.

"I don't like that you're alone," he'd said a month after Ernest's death. "This is a fishing village and you practically live at the seaside. There are many rough sailors pouring onto our shores every day. It's just a matter of time before they begin to notice that you're unattached. I can't protect you when you're on the other side of the village."

As much as she'd wanted to retain her independence, her brother's words made her change her mind. It was true that she was already the object of men's attention, and they refused to let her mourn in peace. It didn't matter that she was still dressing in her mourning garments, dark clothes that shouldn't have drawn any attention to her, but it was her clear, baby blue eyes and golden hair that always made men take a second and third look at her, even in her drab clothes.

What made matters worse was that the cottage she and Ernest would have lived in, had he not died, was in the direct path of the route to the seaside. That was the route that sailors and fishermen used, and it put her in danger. More than once after Ernest's death she'd awakened to find someone trying to break into her cottage. Her screams had brought the neighbours out to see what was happening. When one of them whispered to Miles what was happening, he'd insisted on her coming to live further offshore with them.

Coming to live in her brother's home had created a myriad of new problems with her sister-in-law. With a sigh, she turned to the midwife.

"Is there anything I can do to help?"

"Yes, if you don't mind washing the soiled linens."

"I don't mind at all," Anne said in a soft voice, gathering everything in the pile and showing no distress or revulsion at the stench of blood and human waste, signs of the age-old battle to bring new life into the world that had taken place in this room. "I'll take these down to the cove and clean them," she said as she left.

Trudy finished putting her tools together, then stood and looked at her latest patient.

"It's not my place to say this, but you didn't have to hiss at your sister-in-law. This is the time for you to count on her help and not push her aside. You need help with your baby, and she is here to provide it for you."

"You're right," Jill glared at her, "It's not your place to say anything, and I'll thank you to mind your own business and not interfere in the matters of my family."

"Pardon me, Mrs. Cotton," Trudy pursed her lips, picked up her satchel, and walked to the door. "When will I get my money?"

"When my husband gets back from the mines, I'll see that he brings your money," she said dismissively and went back to gazing at her adorable new-born daughter.

2

AMAZING TIES

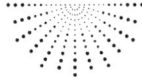

"**S**alome Victoria Cotton, get in here at once," Jill stood at the doorway, arms at her waist. "What do you think you're doing out there?"

"Mama, I'm helping Aunt Anne gut the fish she brought from the shore," three-year-old Sally said. She was such a beautiful child that people often stopped to stare at her. With her milky white skin, even though she spent a lot of time out in the sun, her deep blue eyes and golden hair, she was a child any mother would be proud of. Jill was a doting mother, though the child had somewhat of a rebellious streak in her, even though she was still so young.

"Don't go soiling your clothes. Come in at once and leave that dirty work to the ones who have nothing better to do."

"No," Sally said firmly, "I'm helping Aunt Anne."

"Did you dare say no to me?" Jill fumed, rushing out of the house. She came to a dead stop when she noticed her husband at the small gate watching her. Theirs was the only house with a picket fence among the other cottages that made up this middle-class section of the seaside village. It wasn't that those who lived here were well-to-do, it was that they chose to live what Anne Cotton called pretentious lives. The neighbours' wives were just as snobbish as her sister-in-law.

"Papa," Sally spotted her father, forgot what she'd been doing, and rushed to him. Miles Cotton didn't care that his three-year-old daughter smelled like a fisherman. He dropped his pickaxe and scooped her into his arms, laughing happily. He swung her in the air, and she screamed with joy. "Papa, welcome home," the child said when he placed her on his hip and smiled down at her. The love between father and daughter was intense.

"And that's the reason why I always hurry to get back home," Miles smiled at his sister, whom, he noted, looked exhausted. Then his eyes took in his wife's smart appearance and his lips tightened, but he didn't say a word.

"Papa, what did you bring me?" Sally had her plump arms around her father's neck.

"This," he put one hand into his pocket and pulled out a small green stone. "This is for you," he said, placing it in her dirty hand. "No putting it in your mouth," he warned when she would have done just that.

"Thank you, Papa," Sally wriggled in her father's arms, and he put her down. She ran to her aunt rather than her mother. "See what Papa has brought me," she said excitedly.

"It's very beautiful," Anne agreed and cast a quick glance at her sister-in-law, whose face was tight with disapproval, and there was anger in her eyes.

No one in their fishing village could understand why Sally loved her aunt more than her mother. The little girl followed Anne all over the place, and because they had the same golden hair and deep baby blue eyes, people often mistook them for mother and daughter. This irked Jill to no end, because she was a brunette and had hazel eyes. Sally had taken after her father's side of the family, and Jill hated being reminded of the fact whenever she looked at her sister-in-law.

"Salome, come here at once," Jill called out, and the child dragged her steps as she responded to her mother's summons. "What did I tell you about playing outside and in the dirt?"

Miles frowned at his wife. "Anne is only teaching her how to clean the fish. Every child in this village, and indeed other seaside regions, cuts their teeth on learning how to clean fish and prepare it for cooking."

"My Salome is made for better things than just ending up as a fishwife," Jill said casting a look of disdain at her sister-in-law. "I don't want Sally learning bad habits from worthless people."

"My ancestors were all fishermen," Miles said in a quiet voice, "I, too, am a fisherman at heart, but there's a little more money to be made in the coal mines. Still, I intend to stop working at the mines when I have enough money to buy my own trawler. That's the only reason I'm not on the high seas, where I should be right now."

Jill made a rude sound that shocked Anne. "Don't make such rude sounds in front of Sally," Miles said, "Sally, go to your aunt."

"No, I don't want my child to end up like a scruffy vagabond."

But Miles had had enough. "Sally, go to your Aunt Anne. Your mother and I have some things to talk about," and he gently but firmly pushed his wife into the house.

Sally stood looking at the closed door and then with a sigh trudged back to her aunt.

"Why are they always fighting?" the little girl asked, and Anne gave her a loving look.

"Grown-ups are always talking in loud voices," she said for want of something better to say. "They are not fighting, just talking loudly."

"Does Mama hate Papa?"

"No," Anne said hurriedly, horrified at the child's words. "Sally, you're too young to concern yourself with such matters. Now, can we carry on gutting the fish? I promise to fry you some of it."

The child's face brightened, her parents' spat momentarily forgotten.

～

"If I catch you going outside again, I'll break your legs," Marie Winchester hissed at her six-year-old son. "I told you that I don't want you going outside to play. You're very weak and delicate and playing with that riff raff out there will expose you to all manners of diseases."

Oliver Winchester stood there with his head bowed. More than anything, he wanted to go outside and play. It was a warm spring day, and he could hear the sounds of laughter as the servants' children played in the backyard. His older brother and sister were also outside playing, and he raised his eyes to his mother, chin quivering.

"But Mama, Kent and Maeve are playing outside. Why can't I go to them?"

"I'll backhand you," Marie hissed, and Oliver flinched. "Insolent boy, do you dare to question me?"

"No, Mama, "Oliver was trembling visibly. He cast a glance at his father, whose face was buried behind the newspaper. It was clear that he would get no help from there, and he hung his head.

"Go to your bedchamber and don't come out until I tell you to," she pushed him out of the parlour. "If I catch you wandering around the house like a lost cat, I'll box your ears until they turn black and blue. Do you hear me?"

"Yes, Mama," Oliver ran up the flight of stairs and down the corridor to his bedroom, which overlooked the backyard. Dashing the tears away, he stood at the window and gazed longingly at the sight below. There were about ten children of all ages, including his brother and sister, and they seemed so happy.

One of the children caught sight of him and pointed at him. The game paused, and the other children all waved, save for his brother and sister. Oliver didn't dare wave back because he knew that his siblings would report the action to his parents, and he would get a lashing.

He withdrew and sat on his narrow cot. Sadness filled the little boy's heart as he thought about why his parents didn't seem to like him. Even though he was still very young, he could tell that the way he was treated was different from his siblings. It wasn't just that he wasn't allowed to go out and play. It also had to do with his bedroom, and he looked around. Apart from the small cot he slept in there was also an old closet that had his clothes, all of them having been handed down to him when Kent outgrew them. Oliver had never been bought any new clothes, and he never dared to ask for any.

Unlike those rooms that his siblings occupied, which had been painted in bright colours, Oliver's bedroom had dark walls and a single small window. The single curtain was frayed and dusty because no one had ever taken it down for a wash, at least not that he could recall. What the child didn't know was that in decades past, this had been the governess's room, as it was attached to the nursery. The interconnecting door had been long sealed up, so Oliver had no access to the room next door, which belonged to his brother. Maeve's room and two guest rooms were across the hall, and further down was the master bedroom, which his parents shared.

He had no toys to play with or books to read. The governess who gave his siblings their lessons always sent him away from the schoolroom, but he was a curious child who hadn't yet learnt what fear was. Since he had no friends to play with, he found ways of amusing himself, and one of them was by wandering around the dark corridors of the Manor when no one was about.

A few days ago, as he'd been playing under his bed and hiding from his bully of a brother, he had discovered a loose panel in the wall. Surreptitiously pushing it aside, he'd discovered that it opened into a narrow passage. Because he hadn't wanted his mother or siblings to discover his secret, he had waited until night-time when everyone was asleep. Then taking a candle and match box, he'd slipped into the passage and was careful to count his steps. On that first night, he hadn't wandered far for fear of getting lost in the wall and no one ever finding him. It was a terrifying thought for a child of six years, and he had returned to his bedroom, heart pounding.

The passage was wide and high enough for a grown-up to walk upright, and he wondered who had put it there. Every day he explored a little further, and last night his wanderings had brought him to a narrow staircase at the end of the passage. It was clear to him that this passage went right round the house both on the first and also ground floors. Someone had gone to great pains to hide it, and he doubted that Maeve or Kent, or even his parents, knew of the existence of this passage. As he'd stood at the rickety staircase leading to the ground floor, he thought he heard a low moaning sound, and he hurried to his bedroom, shutting the panel, and lay trembling in the dark for he'd dropped the candle in his haste to flee from what he believed was a ghost.

Now as he sat in his forlorn room, the one thought in his young mind was that the house must be haunted. He once again walked to the window and looked out into the courtyard. He made sure to stand behind the drapes so no one would see him.

Excited yapping made him lean forward, and he sighed. His parents had brought two puppies home for his brother and sister about a week ago. Oliver had dared to ask for a pet and received a tongue lashing from his mother.

"Who do you think you are?" She'd shouted at him, and he'd seen the malicious looks on his sibling's faces. They always enjoyed his humiliation, and he wondered why they had changed toward him so much, especially Maeve. Oliver remembered that when he was younger, Maeve would carry him everywhere and play with him. She had loved him, or so he'd thought, but now all that had changed, and she acted as if she detested him]. "Do you think you're the Queen of England's husband to demand things in this house? Be glad you have a roof over your head and food to eat."

Oliver sighed as he leaned his small forehead on the window. Then he frowned and listened keenly. Something seemed to be scratching the wall, and he looked around but saw nothing. Since his room had the barest of necessities, he could see all the walls save for under the bed and closet. He bent down to peek under his bed and still saw nothing.

Heart pounding, he crawled under the bed and slid the panel open. Something furry shot into the room, startling him and he gave a small cry of alarm, but this turned into a smile when he saw that it just a kitten.

"Come here, Kitty," he said, shutting the panel and crawling from under the bed. The little kitten ran to him and rubbed itself against his thighs as he knelt, and he giggled, staring at it in childlike wonder. "Where did you come from?" he sat down and the cat purred contentedly, climbing onto his lap and cuddling close to his small body. "I'll give you a name, and you are now mine." He laughed when the cat nuzzled his neck, tickling him. "Tubby is what I'll name you." The cat was brown and had a white streak around its neck like a tie. "You sure are a beautiful little thing," he said.

His heart fell when he thought about how his mother would react if she ever found out about his new friend. "We have to keep you hidden because Mama will never let you stay with me," he said, listening for any footsteps in the hallway. His mother loved keeping him locked up in his bedroom, and then she would check on him every few minutes to find out what he was doing. "Tubby, you'll have to learn how to hide so that no one will ever find you."

As if to prove his words, he heard hurried footsteps coming toward his bedroom and the door was thrust open. "What are you doing sitting on the floor? Do you think I employ the servants to take care of only you? If you make those clothes dirty, you'll do your own laundry."

"I'm sorry, Mama," Oliver was trembling because he was afraid of what his mother would do if she spotted the kitten.

"Get into bed right now.;. You you can be sure that there's no lunch or dinner for you for being an insolent boy," she hissed as she slammed the door and left. He felt the tears in his eyes but quickly dashed them away when he realised that his mother hadn't seen the cat.

"Tubby, where are you?" He called out in a soft voice as he pulled back his threadbare blanket and slipped into bed. His mother would most certainly return to make sure that he had obeyed his instructions, and he didn't want to get slapped or hissed at. "Tubby?"

The cat didn't show up, and Oliver felt the tears falling. He was hungry and hadn't eaten much for breakfast because Kent had grabbed the pancakes off his plate and devoured most of them then cast the leftovers back. Sleep wouldn't come, and just as he was wondering where his friend had gone, he felt something jump onto the bed and he sat up, heart pounding.

A smile broke out on his face when he saw his friend. "What's this?" Oliver reached for the small sack the cat had in its mouth. Tubby dropped the sack on the bed, and then cuddled up next to Oliver. He took the sack and opened it, then grinned. There was an apple and a ham sandwich. "Tubby, where did you get this? Are you a ghost or are you real?" He asked as he slipped his surprise gift under his pillow and turned to look at the cat. "What kind of a cat are you, appearing and disappearing without anyone else seeing you? Or am I just imagining that you're real?" But the food was real and after he'd devoured it and then hidden the small sack, he lay back and fell asleep, his small stomach replete for now.

3

CHANGING LIFE

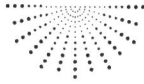

From the moment Sally woke up, she knew that something was different. For one, she wasn't in her small but warm cot, and secondly, she could see the stars in the sky.

"Sally, be still," she heard her aunt's voice whispering in her ear. "Don't make a sound, okay?" Sally nodded, wondering why they were playing hide and seek at night. Then she wrinkled her nose as she smelled something funny. It was as though something was burning but she couldn't tell what it was. Her eyes hurt and she quickly closed them.

Burying her face in her aunt's chest, she soon fell asleep again. When she next woke up, she found that she was still in her aunt's arms, but this time they were in the village church.

"Poor thing," she overheard someone say, "It's so sad that she's lost her parents at such a tender age." Three-year-old Sally barely paid attention to the voices around her. All she knew was that this wasn't home.

"Aunt Anne?"

"Yes, my darling?"

"Where is Papa?" she thought she heard her aunt sniff as if she were crying. Pulling slightly away the child looked up, "Why are you crying?"

"I've got something in my eye," Anne rubbed her red eyes. "Go back to sleep."

"I'm hungry," she put her thumb in her mouth. Sally rarely sucked her thumb. The only time she did that was when she was afraid. Looking around, she could barely make out who the other people were, but she could tell that there were many of them. She snuggled deeper into her aunt's arms and closed her eyes again.

"Sally," someone was shaking her awake, but she didn't want to open her eyes. "Sally, open your eyes," the voice was firmer and she reluctantly opened her eyes. This time she found that she was lying in a small cot. But wait, this wasn't her cot because it was more comfortable and didn't smell funny. Her mattress back at home was old and usually smelled musty. Sally sat up and noticed her aunt seated on a chair next to the cot. But it was her eyes which caught the child's attention. There was so much sadness in them.

"Do you want something to eat?" Anne rose to her feet and picked up her niece. "Come, Mrs. Ferguson has prepared some oatmeal porridge."

"Where is Papa?" Sally looked around but didn't see her father. She always woke up to her loving father standing by her bedside waiting to kiss her before he left for work. For as long as her young mind could remember, her father had never once left for work without waking her up if need be, just to give her a kiss and tell her to be a good girl. But today he wasn't there, and a frown marred her small face. "Pa?" she looked around as her aunt carried her out of the room. "Where is my Pa?"

Anne bit back a sob and entered the large kitchen, which was bustling with activity. There were three or four women running around preparing meals in large pots, and the delicious aromas wafted in the air, tickling the little girl's nose. A plump matronly woman walked up to them with a broad smile on her face. Sally watched as she wiped her thick arms on the blue apron around her massive waist.

"Little Sally, you must be hungry," she held her arms out and Sally slipped into them, putting her head on the woman's motherly shoulder. The child had no idea that the two women shared a sorrowful look over her small head.

"Come, let me get you something to eat," the vicar's wife said, placing the child on a highchair, which had belonged to her now-grown children. She bustled around the kitchen, and soon Sally was drinking warm milk and eating a delicious pie.

Once replete the child looked around her, "Aunt Anne, where is Papa?"

"He can't be with us right now," Anne said, her voice a hoarse whisper as she cast a helpless look in Mrs. Ferguson's direction. "He has gone away."

"Will he come later?"

"Sally," the vicar's wife interrupted, "I have some fruit cake for you," and she placed a thick slice in front of the child. Sally momentarily forgot about her parents as she attacked the piece of cake. The women in the kitchen looked at each other, knowing what was going on but choosing not to say anything. This was a private moment and they were only privy to it because they were helping out in the kitchen.

Anne tried not to pay attention to their pitying glances because she had to be strong for her little niece.

"The little one eats as if she hasn't had anything for a while," Mrs. Ferguson observed. "And you're just bones in clothes," she told Anne.

Anne didn't want to say anything bad about her sister-in-law, who would never be able to defend herself now that she was gone forever.

"If I didn't know better, I'd say your sister-in-law has been starving you. But since I know your brother always brought enough food home, it must be that you're the kind of person who remains small all her life."

Anne stared hungrily at Sally's cake, wishing she could have even a bite.

"Here," Mrs. Ferguson passed her a pie and a cup of tea. "You look like you really need this."

"Thank you," Anne whispered softly as she fell upon the fare. It was soon gone, but her stomach still felt empty.

"Aunty Anne,"

"Yes, my love?"

"Here is some of my cake," Sally passed the remaining piece which Anne soon gobbled down, ignoring their hostess's strange look.

$\backsim$

"My love," Amelia Ferguson told her husband later that evening as they were in their bedchamber at the vicarage. "I think that woman was starving these two," she said. "You should have seen the way they were looking at the food, as if they've never seen something like that before. Yet Miles Cotton was a good father and he never skimped on groceries or providing for his family."

"Why would you think Miss Cotton and Little Sally were starved?" Reverend John Ferguson, who was in charge of the small vicarage, put his official robes away and turned to look at his wife.

"You should have seen the way they fell upon the snacks and then food that I gave them," she shook her head, looking disturbed. "I always said that woman was no good and didn't want Miles to marry her. The poor boy was deeply in love with the pretty face, but her heart held no substance. It was always my fear that she would one day run away with one of those visiting salesmen that she liked spending money on, buying worthless trinkets instead of feeding her family."

"Dear wife," John walked over to his wife and kissed her cheek, "Let's not speak ill of the dead because they are not here to defend themselves."

"But-"

"Sh!" Reverend John put a finger over his wife's lips. "We shall not say anything unkind about Mrs. Jill Cotton. She's dead and gone forever and can't speak for herself. Besides, this isn't the time to talk about the past. We have to start thinking about how to find Miss Anne a place to work and live. It has to be a good household where they will provide sleeping quarters for her, and where she'll be safe. The last thing I want to do is put that poor girl in a household where she'll be molested by the lord of the house or his male guests, and you know that happens quite a lot. Miss Anne has been through so much these past few years that I believe she deserves something good to happen to her."

"What about Sally? What will happen to the little one when Anne has to work?"

"We could keep her with us for a few weeks, until Miss Anne settles down."

Amelia shook her head. "As much as I would like to help out, I don't think Anne will want to leave her little niece behind. Those two are so close that separating them may create a problem. Why, even Jill herself used to complain about how close Anne and Sally are, and believe me, you'll have a good fight on your hands when you bring up such a suggestion."

"Dear good wife, I don't think Miss Anne will protest when we tell her that we can keep the little one until she settles down. Miss Anne is a reasonable young woman, and she will see that what we're suggesting is for her own good as well as that of the child. And Little Sally is too small to be a problem. She'll soon settle down in our household until her aunt can take her back." But the vicar was to find out that separating Anne and Sally wasn't as easy as he'd thought. The moment he made the suggestion, a stubborn look came over Anne's face, and his wife gave him a look that said, "I told you so." He had found her a post as housekeeper with a family in the neighbourhood, and he expected her to jump at the good fortune.

"I'm not leaving my niece behind. Where I go, Sally goes." Anne stood her ground. "She is the only family I have left, and there's no way I'm going to go anywhere without her. If those people won't let me keep Sally, then I don't want that position."

"It's just for a few weeks," Reverend Ferguson tried to convince her, but she only shook her head.

"If you're tired of us staying here at the vicarage, I can always take my niece and leave for London. I know that I will find a post where we can always be together."

"Miss Anne, we will never be tired of having you here because you're like our family. My concern is that the Redwood family doesn't have enough space to accommodate you and Sally. They live less than a mile away, and you can come over and visit with Sally whenever you're free."

"I'm sorry, but what you're asking me to do in not acceptable. If I can't live with my niece then I don't want that position," Anne said and turned away.

A few days later, Mrs. Ferguson found a cook's position over at the large manor belonging to the Winchesters. They were the wealthiest family in Potter's Cove, and Amelia felt that the position would be ideal for Anne.

"Anne," Amelia tried to convince the girl, "Mrs. Winchester is a wealthy woman, and I believe she pays her staff well. You'll be happy over there."

"If you say she pays her staff well, then why did her cook leave?"

"The woman was quite old and needed to retire. They need someone new and young enough to follow instructions. Mrs. Winchester told me that Old Wilhelmina never paid attention to instructions and had started burning their meals. According to Mrs. Winchester, she nearly burnt down the house when she fell asleep in the kitchen and let the fat splatter all over the floor. It was quite a mess."

"But will she allow me to have Sally with me? If you're talking about the Winchester estate, I happen to know that they have cottages for their workers. Will she give me one of those?"

"I felt that you would be safer living in the servants' quarters at the manor, seeing that you're a young and single woman. Those cottages are built for the married servants and their families."

"I'm a married woman and I have Sally so that makes us a family. If Mrs. Winchester will agree to let us have one of the cottages, then I'm ready to start work tomorrow."

"What if she says all the cottages are full but she can provide a room for you at the manor?"

"I don't think she will let me stay with Sally at the manor, Mrs. Ferguson."

"Like my husband said, we can keep Sally with us until you settle down. I'm sure once you're working for Mrs. Winchester, you can find a way of getting your own place. What do you think?"

Anne merely shrugged, "Then Sally and I will find another place to live and work. If it's all right with you, we will leave tomorrow morning."

"But where will you go?" Amelia cried out while silently pleading for her husband to intervene, "You don't have any money."

"What my wife says is true, Miss Anne," the vicar said, "We will take good care of Sally until you're able to find a better position where you can live with her."

"I don't think you're listening to me," Anne said in a firm voice, "Where I go, Sally goes. If those people won't let me keep Sally, who is now like my own child, then I want nothing to do with them. And please don't try to make me accept their terms, for it's only going to irritate me."

When the vicar and his wife realized that nothing they said would get the young woman to change her mind, they left her alone.

But two days later, Reverend Ferguson came to the house, a broad smile on his face.

"Mrs. Winchester is willing to give you an old cottage on the estate where you and Sally will live. Now will you accept the position?"

"Right away," Anne beamed.

~

While the Winchester Manor was quite impressive, the cottage that was allocated to Anne was nothing more than a rundown shack. But at least it was just a few feet away from the main Manor, and with all the guards who patrolled the estate, it was quite safe. Though Reverend Ferguson was worried that the guards might molest Anne, he believed that her employer would keep her safe, for he had made her promise to do so.

"Will you be happy here?" Reverend Ferguson asked as he looked around the single room. It was large enough and already had a bed and a small table with two chairs, and a chest of drawers in one corner. There was also a grate where Anne could do her cooking, and three old blackened pots had been provided for that purpose. "It's really bare."

"It's our own home, nonetheless," Anne said as she stood in the middle of the room. "It may be old, but the foundation is sturdy, and as soon as I get my first wages, I'll be able to buy us warmer beddings and maybe a new mattress."

"I'll come by tomorrow and make sure the shingles are properly fastened, and I don't like that this door looks so weak. With one feeble kick, someone can have it down and then attack you."

"Reverend Ferguson," Anne didn't want the man trying to convince her to live in the manor. "Sally and I will be all right. In the evenings, I will make sure to push the table and our bed against the door to prevent anyone who wishes to gain entrance forcefully."

"Still, I'll come by tomorrow and make some repairs to the house. You're a very stubborn young woman, but I believe you'll be all right."

"Thank you, sir."

Anne started working at the manor the very next day, and she grimaced as she walked into the pantry. It looked like it hadn't been cleaned in ages, and there was a funny smell. Her new mistress couldn't be bothered to show her what she needed to do, but Anne was a fast learner and soon got the hang of things. The only other servant who came into the kitchen was a young woman nearly her age, but she turned her nose up at Anne.

"So you're the new cook," she said haughtily, walking around the kitchen. "Mrs. Winchester has told me to come and show you what needs to be done."

"Thank you, you're so kind," Anne said politely.

"Groceries are brought in every week on Fridays, and you have to make sure that they last for seven days. The old woman who was here before you was a mess and would steal food. If you want to keep your job here, then you'll never steal from this house, is that clear?"

"Yes, Ma'am."

"Good. Now do you have any questions?"

"What time are meals served, and how many of them should I prepare every day, and for how many people?"

"Mrs. Winchester and her husband have three children, so meals for five. She likes breakfast to be ready by seven in the morning. Usually you'll serve eggs, bacon, ham, and beans, as well as fresh bread. I hope you know how to bake bread." Anne nodded. "Then there's mid-morning tea which is served with scones or cake. Lunch is at one o'clock, and you should never be late for this. Mr. and Mrs. Winchester are very busy people and don't stand for slackness. At four o'clock you'll serve more tea, and dinner is promptly at seven. Do you have any more questions?"

Anne shook her head, even though her mind was whirling with questions. She didn't want the other woman to give her haughty answers.

"One more thing," the woman said, "As a cook, you're not allowed to set food outside this kitchen into the main house."

"Then who will serve the food?"

"I'll do it, and then there's Pauline, who will come in later. She will assist you in the kitchen, but you have to be careful because she doesn't know how to cook. Her work is to clean the pots and pans and maybe help you with chopping, dicing, and cutting of food, but never cooking. She will also carry food through the dining hall, and I will serve the Winchesters. If Mrs. Winchester finds that you've made Pauline cook any of the meals, you'll soon be tossed out on your ear."

"Thank you for helping me get settled in," Anne smiled but the woman didn't return her gesture. It was with much relief that Anne watched her walk out of the kitchen, and as the woman's footsteps faded on the wooden tiles, she breathed easier. She hadn't even told Anne her name, so Anne wasn't sure how was she supposed to address her.

Sally had been hiding in the large flowery bush right outside the kitchen, and once the other woman had left, she crept into the kitchen. "Aunt Anne, will we live here?"

"We have our own cottage, dear child, but this is where I will work. And Sally, we don't want any trouble, so when I ask you to do something, please do it as fast as possible." Sally nodded. "Now, see that large table in the corner?"

"Yes."

"Go and sit under it and don't move or speak until I come and get you, is that clear?"

"Can I go out to play with the other children I saw there?"

"No, Sally. If these people see you, then they will ask us to leave, and I need to have this position so we can stay in our little house. Or do you want them to tell you to leave so you can go and stay with Mrs. Ferguson?"

"No," Sally said as she slipped under the table, and it was just in time. A young woman entered the kitchen from the outside in quite a flurry.

"Sorry," she said, looking at Anne curiously. "Are you the new cook?"

"Yes. My name is Anne Cotton."

"I'm Pauline Stover." She looked around. "So, they got rid of the old bat after all," she chuckled. "That woman was a terror and I should know."

"How long have you worked in this household?"

"Two years now and let me tell you that in all that time, Mrs. Winchester has never set foot in this kitchen. The old bat wouldn't let her cross the threshold but did as she wanted. At first when I came in, the food wasn't so bad, but it got progressively worse. I'm just glad the woman is gone." Pauline reached into the pantry for an old apron. "Make sure you always have an apron on, or Miss High and Mighty will flay you."

Anne frowned, "Who is that?"

"Haven't you met Emelda, who feels like she's the queen of this palace? She is the housekeeper and another one who is terrible at her work. But Mrs. Winchester keeps her here because Mr. Winchester claims she is his cousin," Pauline snorted. "Cousin indeed!"

Anne realised that she was dealing with a woman who loved to gossip, and that was one of the vices that could cost her this position. She had to get her to stop gossiping, and hard work was the only way . "Would you be so kind as to help me clean up the pantry?"

4

VALLEY OF SHADOWS

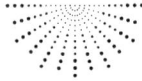

hree Years Later

TOliver woke up with a start and realized that there was a weight pressing down on his chest. Panicked, he flailed out with his arms, his small fists pounding against the body that was pressing him down. The room was in darkness, and he couldn't see who it was, though he could hear the heavy breathing. The person placed a hand over his mouth and nose as if trying to suffocate him. Just when he felt he was about to lose consciousness, a chilling shriek burst out in the dark, and suddenly the weight fell off his chest and he heard someone hiss in pain.

As Oliver lay there, heart pounding in the dark, he heard the person stumble toward the door, fling it open, and then was gone.

The ten-year-old sat up, frightened beyond words, but then he felt the small fur ball wriggle closer to him. "Tubby," he whispered, holding the kitten close. "You saved my life," the child said. He wished he could call out for his mother, but he knew she wouldn't come. And even if she did, she would only end up whipping him because of having disturbed her sleep.

As fat tears rolled down his small face, Oliver wondered why his mother hated him so much. The way his parents behaved towards him was so different from the way they treated Kent, his fifteen-year-old brother, and Maeve, his twelve-year-old sister. He couldn't recall ever receiving any words of praise from his parents. And all Kent and Maeve did was to tease him mercilessly, hitting him when whenever he met with them along the corridors. They often tripped him, and more so when he was carrying anything. Then they would just stand there and laugh at him. Many nights he went to bed hungry, because if he spilled his food, his mother never allowed him to have any more. Instead, she berated him for carelessness, whipped him soundly, and sent him hungry to bed. If he didn't know better, it was as though his family was out to crush his very soul and end his life.

"Tubby, I think I should run away," he buried his small face in the cat's fur. "But I don't know where to go."

The cat licked his face and he giggled because it tickled. Even in the midst of his despair, this little friend who had come to him from nowhere three years ago was always there to comfort him. What's more, once in a while Tubby would bring him something to eat. Where she got thetidbits she brought him, he would never know, but he wasn't one to look a gift horse in the mouth.

Tonight, his furry friend had saved him from suffocation, and though he suspected that it was Kent who had tried to murder him as he slept, he couldn't tell anyone. No one would believe him, and Maeve would only defend their older brother. Those two were as thick as thieves insofar as hatching up their sinister plots to make his life miserable. If he had someplace to go, he would have run away a long time ago. But even then, he loved his home, even though its other inhabitants were cruel beings. There was something about this old Manor that tugged at his heartstrings, and he knew that if he were to ever leave, he'd miss this place terribly.

"Tubby, what am I going to do?"

❧

"Sally, please don't go wandering around the house, okay?" The child nodded, her thumb in her mouth. "Sit in your corner under the table and don't move; do you hear me?"

"Yes, Aunt Anne," Sally crawled into the space under the large kitchen table that had been pushed against the wall. It was quite dark but Sally wasn't afraid of the darkness. She'd been like a little phantom because Aunt Anne didn't want anyone to find out who she really was. She would slip in and out of the house whenever she could, but ultimately she ended up under the large table. It was a wonder to the child that no one apart from her aunt ever bothered to look under the table.

"Here, eat this while you wait for lunch, and stay silent," her aunt held out a thick cookie.

Sally took the cookie from her aunt's hand and crawled back into her corner. When she was done eating, she lay down on the old shawl her aunt had spread out for her, and within minutes she was asleep.

She woke up to something tickling her nose and giggled when she opened her eyes and saw two luminous green eyes staring at her.

"Who are you?" she whispered, reaching out a hand, quite unafraid. "Come closer, I won't hurt you."

"Sally, are you awake?" Her aunt came, knelt in front of the table, and peered under it. This was the perfect hiding spot, for no one ever bothered to check under here—no one being Pauline, the only other person who spent time in the vast kitchen. For some reason the little girl didn't want her aunt to know about her new friend, so she sat up and moved forward, willing the cat to remain hidden.

"Yes, can I come out now?"

"No, but here is your lunch. Remember you can't come out until it is evening, and we have to go home. I don't want anyone to see you because then we will get into trouble."

Loud footsteps came down the corridor toward the kitchen, and Anne scrambled to her feet, hurriedly returning to her place behind the chopping table.

Sally drew back into the darkness and felt around for her friend, but the cat was gone. She felt a little bit sad but had a feeling that her new friend would be back.

"Why isn't lunch ready and served?" A sharp female voice made Sally pause from eating. She knew it was the mistress of the house. She came down to the kitchen twice a day, and each time she found something to be angry about, and one time she had even slapped Aunt Anne.

"I'm sorry Ma'am, the table is already set, and I was serving it while Pauline is bringing the first course in."

"Hurry up," the woman turned and left, and Sally let out the breath she'd been holding. At least she hadn't struck Aunt Anne today.

The scullery maid even seemed unaware of her existence, but Sally knew that it was because she was rather a scatterbrain who loved to gossip and just laze around. Each morning they would come in from their small, one-room cottage when it was still very dark. Sally would crawl under the table to her corner and continue sleeping while her aunt prepared breakfast. When the day was lighter and the weather fair, Sally would slip out and wander around the large estate, taking care not to get into trouble. Then she would return to the kitchen and back to her spot.

In the evenings Anne would help the scullery maid wash the dishes and clean the kitchen. Once Pauline, the scullery maid, had gone to her small room next to the pantry, Sally would slip out and they would head home.

Sally was getting bored even though she was sure that she had now made a new feline friend. The child was curious about where the cat had come from. No one talked of a cat living in the house. She'd seen the two dogs owned by the children of the manor, but never a cat.

Two days later, as she was resting under the table, her friend returned, and she pulled the cat close. It didn't seem to want to cuddle but kept walking to the door and back, and the child felt like it was telling her to follow it.

"Where do you go when you leave here?" she whispered to the cat, crawling after it. It was mid-morning, and her aunt and Miss Pauline were busy at the large sink, their backs turned toward her. She darted after the cat and found herself in a dark hallway. The cat seemed to be waiting for her, and she followed it up the narrow stairs at the end of the corridor to a dark landing. The cat then pushed open a door, and after a brief hesitation, Sally entered the room.

"Who are you?" A boy with dark hair and deep blue eyes asked her, "Where did you come from?"

"My name is Sally," she looked at the kitten, "I followed your kitten."

"This is Tubby, and my name is Oliver." The two children stood there looking at each other without saying a word for a while. "Tubby is too big to be called a kitten anymore."

"She is pretty."

"Who?" Owen looked at Sally in puzzlement.

"The cat," Sally drew further into the room, "Is she yours?"

"Yes," there was a funny note in Oliver's voice, "But she found me. Do you live in this house? You're too small to be walking around alone. Is your mother here in this house with you?"

Sally clasped her hands behind her back and shook her head. "Auntie Anne is my mother now."

"What do you mean?" Oliver asked, "How can your aunt be your mother also?"

Sally raised her small shoulders and then dropped them down. "My Mama and Papa went away and then we came here to this big house."

"So, you live here then?"

"No, we have our own cottage, but Aunt Anne cooks in the big kitchen downstairs." Sally walked around the room. "Do you sleep here alone?"

"Yes," Oliver looked around the room, "Why do you ask?"

Sally put her face to her side and shook her head. "It's so empty."

Oliver smiled wryly, "I'm used to it."

"Why don't you ever go outside to play with the other children? Sometimes when Miss Pauline and my aunt mother are busy, I come out of the kitchen and hide in the bushes to watch the other children playing. But I've never seen you out there."

"I can't go outside because my mother won't let me. She says I will get sick, so I have to stay inside my room. Do you have brothers and sisters?"

"No, do you?"

"Yes, Kent and Maeve."

Sally scrunched her little face. "I think I have seen them. Why don't you play with them?"

Oliver shrugged, "They don't like me to play with them."

"Will you play with me then? I also don't have anyone to play with. Aunt Annie makes me sit under the table in the kitchen so no one will see me."

"How did you get here then?"

Sally covered her lips with her small hands and giggled. "I told you that I followed

Tubby. She brought me here."

"Did you use the wide staircase in the lobby?"

Sally shook her head. "I followed Tubby down the long corridor. It was really dark, but I wasn't scared. Tubby showed me where to go."

Oliver sat on the bed and reached for the cat which was dozing on the bed. "Well, thank you for coming. No one else has come to see me on my birthday."

"Is it your birthday today?" Oliver nodded. "How old are you?"

"Ten years old."

"Will your mother bring you a cake? My aunt said that she will bake me a cake on my birthday. Will your mother tell Aunt Anne to bake you a cake?"

Oliver shook his head and looked very sad. "I haven't had a cake in a long time."

"Why?"

"You ask too many questions. Go away now," he turned and lay on his bed, cuddling the cat.

Sally stood there for a long while; then she nodded and opened the door, but just stood there confused. The corridor was long, and she couldn't remember how she had gotten to Oliver's room. Then she felt the cat at her ankles and Tubby went out, leading the way. Sally was giggling as she followed the cat down the dark and narrow stairs and slipped back into the kitchen without anyone seeing her.

"Thank you," she whispered to the cat. "Now go back to Oliver, because he's really sad."

5

UNUSUAL FRIENDSHIP

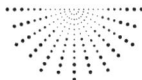

"**O**liver! Oliver!" He felt someone shaking him, and he shot up from sleep. "You were crying," Sally told him.

"No, I was not," he told her sullenly, but she gave him a look that told him she knew he was lying.

"Your face is covered in tears."

He put his hand on his face and it came away wet. He was slightly embarrassed at having been caught like this.

"What do you want?" His voice was rough, but Sally didn't seem intimidated at all. This was her friend of three years, and she was used to him sometimes being brash.

"Remember? You told me it's your birthday today," she told him, then pointed at the small package she had placed on his table. "Aunt Annie baked a cake, and I asked her for a big piece; then I hid it so I could bring it to you."

A grin broke out on Oliver's face, and he quickly got out of bed. "This is for me?"

"Yes, now hurry and eat it before your greedy sister and brother find it." And Oliver proceeded to do just that.

As the days went by, the children's friendship grew. It was a wonder to them that no one else in the household knew of Sally's presence, apart from her aunt. She sneaked in and out of his room and was very careful to never get caught. Oliver had even named her "the pretty phantom," and she liked it. He had told her to always wait for Tubby to lead her to the room because the cat seemed to know when people weren't around.

"My birthday is in two months and I'll be turning six, "Sally announced one morning, holding up six fingers. Then something struck her, "Where's Tubby?" Oliver was licking the cream off his fingers from another piece of cake that she'd brought him and ignored the question. "Oliver, is Tubby lost?"

"No." He looked at her face a long time and then seemed to come to a decision. Sally had been his friend and companion for a while now, and he trusted her. And not only that, but each time she sneaked into his bedroom, she would bring him something to eat. Sometimes it was a piece of cake or pie and once in a while she would even bring hard sugar candy. The girl never came empty handed, and he counted himself really lucky to have a good friend like her, and Tubby too.

Sally stood there rocking from side to side, and then dread filled her heart. What if Oliver's wicked siblings had harmed Tubby? Oliver had told her about how twice he'd woken up to find someone choking him, and twice Tubby had saved his life. She would jump at his assailant and the person would flee. He suspected that it was his siblings, but he was too afraid of their mother to report them.

"Oliver, did someone hurt Tubby?"

"No, she is okay."

"Why isn't she here then?"

"She goes hunting for rats, and I know where she goes, but you have to promise me something."

"What?"

"I'll show you something, but you have to be very quiet, and you can never tell anyone."

"I promise."

"Good," Oliver fell on his knees and then slipped under the bed as an astonished Sally watched him, mouth wide open. "Come on."

"Under the bed?" Was this some sort of new game? "What are you doing under the bed?"

"Just shut up and come down here." She hesitated briefly but decided to follow him. She was surprised to see him slip through a hole in the wall and he urged her to follow him. Just as he was slipping the panel into place, they heard the bedroom door opening.

"Who?" Sally started but he placed a hand over her mouth.

"Oliver," It was his brother Kent, "Where is that little pest?"

"He doesn't seem to be here," Maeve replied. "But I don't think he's gone very far, maybe to the outhouse. See, his bed is unmade."

"I'll skin him alive for leaving the room untidy."

"Or better still, why don't we tell Mama? She can then come and flog him." They laughed unkindly, then walked out of the room, slamming the door behind them.

That's when Oliver scrambled to his feet in the passageway that he'd quite gotten used to. He felt for something on the ground and then Sally saw the flare of a matchstick as Oliver lit a small candle.

"Why do your siblings like beating you up?"

"Because I'm small," he said.

"I'm sorry, "she said, slipping her small hand in his. It was a comforting gesture, and the children stood in the passage for a while. "What are we doing here?"

"Don't talk, Sally. Just follow me," Oliver said as he dropped her hand and led the way. The small candle he had in his hand was flickering, casting shadows along the walls and in front of them. Oliver stopped abruptly and Sally bumped into him.

"Why are you stopping?"

"Because this is the end of the passage," Oliver whispered. "There's a small staircase going down."

"Where does it lead to?"

Oliver raised his shoulders and dropped them. "I don't know, I've never been down there."

Sally peeked over his shoulder. "Can you hear anything?"

"There's a ghost down there," Oliver whispered.

Sally leaned closer to him. "Have you ever seen the ghost?"

"No, but I have heard it sometimes."

"What does it say?"

"Help me."

Something brushed against Sally's feet and she gave a yelp.

"Shh!" Oliver put his hand over her mouth. "That's only Tubby. If you make noise, someone will hear us."

"Let's go back," Sally's voice trembled, "I want to go to Aunt Anne."

"I'm sorry that I frightened you," Oliver said as he led the way back to the room. It was empty and the two children quickly slipped in. Sally was shaking, and she hastened back to the kitchen, slipping in unnoticed.

She crawled to her corner under the large table and raised her knees, putting her head on them.

"Sally," Anne came and crouched to see her niece, "Are you hungry?"

"Yes, Aunt Anne."

"Okay, let me finish serving the main meal and I'll get you something to eat."

As Sally waited for her meal, she wondered if Oliver would come downstairs to the dining room. He'd told her that many times he stayed hungry because no one called him for meals. And during the times that he went to the dining hall, his sister or brother would cause him so much trouble that he'd have to leave the meal halfway.

When Aunt Anne served her some pie and two bananas, she carefully divided the food into two portions and slipped one into her pocket. She then settled down to eat her potion.

Anne went back to her work and thanked God over and over again for having a very lazy scullery maid. Pauline rarely stayed in the kitchen, preferring to either sleep in her room when she should be working, or else she would go out to the stables to flirt with the young men. Rarely was she in the kitchen, and that is how Sally had remained hidden from her sight for so long. Three years in this household, and Anne was as happy as she could be.

Because she was a hard worker, her mistress rarely came to the kitchen to disturb her anymore. As for the housekeeper, the woman seemed to be a queen in her own right, and she also rarely set foot in the kitchen. Emelda, as Anne had found out from Pauline, was Mr. Winchester's mistress, but his wife was none the wiser. Since she rarely bothered with matters that didn't concern her, Anne chose to keep out of Pauline's gossip.

The household had recently acquired two more servants, young women who cleaned the bedchambers and the rest of the house. Karen and Rita were gossips like Pauline, and the three of them sometimes chose to ignore Anne, not that she minded. She was here to work and earn a living for her and Sally, and she was saving money so they could leave for London. Her desire was to find work in one of the nice hotels there, since she was a good cook, and she also wanted Sally to get a good education.

"Aunt Anne," Sally called out to her one evening when they were in their small house.

"Yes, my dear?" She looked up from the dress she was stitching. One thing Anne liked about Pauline was that she was quite generous. Whenever Mrs. Winchester gave her Maeve's old frocks, she would pick out one or two and give them to Anne. Anne would then turn them into small dresses for Sally, who was growing up so fast. She was fast coming to the realisation that they couldn't continue hiding her under the table in the kitchen.

"When will Pa and Ma come back? You told me that they went away. Why haven't they come back? And it's nearly my birthday again."

Anne sighed, putting her sewing aside for the moment. "Sally, do you remember Mr. Walter?"

"Yes, the man who used to take care of the horses at the big stables."

"Do you remember when I told you that he had died and gone to heaven?" The child nodded. "Do you understand that he will never come back again to look after the horses?"

"I saw young Phillip washing the horses," Sally said, and Anne bit back a smile. "He's lazy, that one, and all he does is make faces at Pauline."

"Sally!"

"Aunt Anne, I can't stay under the table every day. Can I stay in the stable with Phillip? He's a lazy oaf but has a good heart."

"Child, who has been filling your head with all this nonsense?"

"I heard Pauline telling Karen that Phillip is an oaf with a good heart, and I think it's because he gives her pretty things. The other day he brought her a lace handkerchief, and she was so happy."

Anne shook her head, at least relieved that she didn't have to explain about Sally's parents. The child knew that they had gone away, but Anne had been wrestling with the idea of telling her about their deaths.

Sally stood up and walked over to her aunt. "Aunt Anne, when will Pa come back? I want to see him."

Anne lifted her and placed her on her knees. "Sally, you're growing up now and understand what death is, don't you?" Sally nodded. "Three years ago, when we went to Mrs. Ferguson's house, it was because our house burnt down."

Sally snuggled close to her aunt as Anne remembered the fateful day that had turned her little niece into an orphan and robbed her of her beloved brother and their home.

As usual, Jill had gone out to gossip with her snotty neighbourhood friends, and she'd taken Sally with her just to show her off, as she always did. Sally was a very intelligent child, and, by the time she was three years old, she could read and had even started writing some words. Her father was so proud of her. He would buy her books and had even encouraged Anne to teach her to read and write, but Jill often interrupted their lessons, dressed the child in fancy clothing, and then went out with her.

The worst thing was that Jill never bought any groceries and, unless Miles did so, there would be no food in the house. Anne had taken to going down to the seaside to scavenge for fish from the traders and fishermen. Whatever she acquired she would bring back and prepare for them all, surprised that Jill would devour the food so greedily without knowing where it had come from.

On the fateful day after Jill returned with Sally, she found that Miles had come back early from the mines, and he was really angry. They quarrelled, and because Anne didn't want Sally to be affected by her parents' fighting, she took the child and told her they were going to the vicarage. Usually when Miles and Jill were fighting, which had become very frequent, Anne would visit Mrs. Ferguson and stay at the vicarage until her brother would come and fetch them. But on that day, he didn't come, and Anne dozed off. They would have stayed at the vicarage until morning but for Mrs. Ferguson's brother, who was a good-for-nothing wastrel. He'd come to visit his sister and was bothering Anne, so she decided to take Sally and go home.

Because she hadn't wanted Richard to follow her, she sneaked out of the house carrying Sally, and when they were close to the house, she saw the large fire. People were running around, and she was too frightened to find out what was going on because she had Sally with her. So, she sat at a distance and watched as five houses burned to the ground. No one knew how the fire had started, but only Miles and Jill perished. The others had managed to get out in a hurry, and the coroner who was called in said that the smoke must have overwhelmed the two of them as they slept, but Anne had her suspicions.

Her brother would never go to sleep without seeing his daughter, and she suspected that Jill must have done something to him, and then weighed down with guilt, had also ended her own life by setting fire to their cottage so no one would ever know the truth. But she didn't tell Sally about her suspicions because she wanted the child to remember her mother well.

Sally sniffed, "So I'll never see Ma and Pa again?"

"We'll see them one day because they are in heaven. They can't come back to us, but we will eventually go to them."

"Will you also go to heaven and leave me, Aunt Anne?"

Anne's hands arms tightened around her niece, "Not for a long, long time. Now sleep. Tomorrow is a busy day for all of us. Sally, I love you, and I will never leave you."

6

THE GHOST

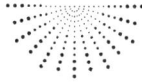

A couple of days later, Oliver decided that it was time for him and Sally to venture further down the passage behind the walls and into the dungeons to find out who or what was down there. She was his friend, and he felt he could trust her. He was also tired of wondering what was going on. As soon as she appeared, as she always did, he told her what he'd decided.

"Sometimes I think there is someone down there in the dungeons calling out to me," he said and looked at her to see if she would mock him. But Sally's face was serious as if she was pondering his words. "I used to be frightened when I heard the voice, but ever since Tubby came to me, I'm no longer afraid. She goes down to the dungeon and nothing bad has happened to her so far, so I guess it's safe."

"Did you say that Tubby often disappears down into the dungeon?"

"I believe so, because where else does she go?"

"Do you think-?" Sally's voice faded.

"What, Sally, what?" There was a new nervous excitement in Oliver's eyes.

"What if we went down there? What if we followed Tubby?"

"Aren't you scared?" He was happy that he didn't have to ask her to go down with him, for he'd been afraid that she would refuse. It wasn't that he was frightened of going alone, because he knew that Tubby would tag along. He just felt that, if there was anything to be discovered in the dungeons, then this was the time to know what it was.

"If Tubby is with us, I know she will protect us." Sally sounded very sure of what she was saying.

"Then let's go."

They slipped through the panel and closed it, then crawled down the passage for a few steps.

"Why are we crawling?" Sally asked, and Oliver giggled. He was ahead of her and stopped, then got to his feet, reaching down and helping her up too. "And where is Tubby?" The passage was dark, but the children had been down this way so many times that they knew the route to the narrow staircase by heart. "Oliver, I don't see Tubby."

"She is right here in front of me."

"What if it's dark down there? How will we see where we're going?"

"Let's go back and get the candle," he suggested, and they turned, but just as he slid the panel open, the door to his bedroom opened. He slid the panel back and only left a small space so the draft wouldn't alert the person in his room that there was an opening in the wall. No one had ever found the panel, and this was his secret hiding place.

"See, I told you that pesky child isn't here. He's probably hiding in the stables," Kent said, sounding frustrated. "No matter how many times I come to this room, I never find him here."

"Let's go, "Maeve said, "We'll watch out for him at lunch time, and then you can beat him up." The two left, slamming the door shut.

"Wait here," Oliver said, scrambling out of the passage. He quickly grabbed the candle from where he had hidden it. His mother never let him have any light, and it was Sally who usually brought him candles.

"Why do they hate you so much?" Sally asked. "I used to wish to have a sister or brother or—even both,—but I'm happy I am alone. Well, I have Aunt Anne."

Oliver simply grimaced and ignored the question she always asked him. He had no real answer for why his siblings were mean to him. "Let's go quickly. Tubby, lead the way."

As if the cat understood her master's instructions, she led the way down the passage once again.

"I don't think these steps have been used in a long time, and they could be broken," Oliver said. "Wait here until I get to the bottom. If I fall you can go and get help."

"Yes," Sally said, holding onto the rickety railing, heart pounding as she watched Oliver carefully descending the creaking steps. She winced and prayed that no one would hear them and come to find out what was going on. She kept her eyes on the flickering candle, and at last he stopped and turned around.

"Come on down, but slowly," and she did as bid. Once she was at his level, she looked around. The walls loomed in the darkness, and the small candle barely lit up the place.

"I don't see a way out," Sally said when she realized that the walls covered all sides. There didn't seem to be a door, and the two children were disappointed, but not for long.

"There must be something like a panel." Oliver insisted. "Where is Tubby?" He looked around and the cat meowed. "There she is," Oliver pointed to one corner of the room. It smelled musty, and Sally wrinkled her nose. Then, to the children's surprise, the cat disappeared from their sight like a ghost. Oliver knelt and then rose to his feet. "There's some space through which I can crawl."

"I'll wait here," Sally wasn't afraid of the dark, but she didn't like being confined in this space. "Hurry and see what is out there."

It was a tight squeeze, but Oliver found himself on the other side of the wall. He was surprised to find a flaming torch on one of the walls. He bent down and urged Sally to join him. This passage was large, and they followed the cat. The place was surprisingly dry, even though it smelled funny.

There were a number of empty cells, and Sally slipped her hand into Oliver's. "Do you think we'll see the ghost? Can we call out?"

"No," he whispered, "Let's just follow Tubby and see where she leads us."

"I'm scared."

"Don't be. Tubby will protect us." There was a slight tremor in Oliver's voice which showed that even he was frightened. Sally didn't know why, but that made her feel slightly better.

"Should we go back?" She asked, looking around to see if anyone or anything could be following them.

"No," Oliver said, "Tubby is still going forward, so let's follow her."

After walking for a short while and passing a second torch, Oliver suddenly stopped.

"Why have you stopped?" Sally bumped into him.

"Tubby entered one of the cells," Oliver pointed. The two children stood there wondering what to do. Tubby dashed out and came to them, circling around their ankles as she meowed.

"I think Tubby wants us to go to the cell," Sally whispered.

"I'm scared."

"But you said Tubby will protect us."

He gave a small nod, and they continued forward. The second torch lit the cell and the two children stared at the creature they found there. When it moved, they screamed in fear and wanted to run away.

"Don't," the hoarse voice said, and they saw that it was a very hairy man who was seated with his back against the wall, his legs stretched out before him. His beard reached his chest, and as for his hair, it went down past his shoulders. It was a thick mane like that of the lions that were in one of Sally's books that she had brought to Oliver. "Can't hurt you," he whispered, but they stood there, shaking in their shoes. Tubby ran up to the man and curled herself on his lap, and he tickled her. "There you are, my little friend. I see you brought people to see me."

That was what made the children draw further into the cell which stunk of bodily waste.

"Who are you?" It was Sally who asked the question. "Why are you sitting on the ground, and why do you look like that?"

The man smiled. "I should ask you that," he said, "Do you live here?"

They nodded, and Oliver squeezed Sally's wrist harder and she winced, trying to pull away but he held fast.

"Oliver, that hurts."

"Sorry," he dropped her hand and she rubbed her wrist, a scowl on her face. "Mister, are you a ghost?"

The man chuckled, but it was more of a rumble. "Come and touch me. I'm not a ghost." Sally stepped forward, but Oliver restrained her.

"Sally don't go close to him. He might hurt you."

She snorted. "If Tubby likes him, then he is a good person. See how Tubby isn't afraid of him." She drew closer and he held out his hand. She touched him then hastily stepped away.

"Don't be afraid."

"Why is your hair so long?" Sally asked as she sat down on her haunches. She noticed the large shackles on his legs and arms, and another around his waist. "Are you a prisoner?"

He smiled at her, and she found that she liked his eyes. He reminded her of someone, but she couldn't remember who it was.

"Where did you come from?" the man looked at them curiously. "How did you get down here?"

Oliver drew closer and joined Sally. "What do you eat down here? And why does this place smell so bad?" He wrinkled his nose.

Sally saw something like shame on the man's face and he looked away. She felt compassion well up within her. His clothes were tattered, and he looked like he was really cold.

"Mister, don't you have a blanket?"

"No, my child. It gets very cold in here, but he comes to light a fire every night."

"Who?" Sally asked, "Why doesn't he bring you a blanket and food?"

The man sighed, "Child, you ask too many questions. Do you have anything to eat?"

Sally remembered that she'd slipped a piece of pie and half a banana in her pocket. She'd intended to give them to Oliver.

"Here," she held them out, but he couldn't raise his hands.

"Throw them on the ground and I will eat from there." Sally did that, and the children were surprised when he stretched himself to his side and ate from the ground, much like Tubby did sometimes. Within seconds her offerings were gone, and he looked at them expectantly.

"That's all we have for now, but I promise to bring you more tomorrow."

7
TROUBLED TIMES

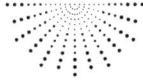

The weeks crept past, and the two children continued to visit the man in the dungeon. They would sit with him for many hours, and each time they left, he looked at them with very sad eyes.

He still wouldn't tell them his name, but they had lost all fear of him. Through talking to him, they had found out that he'd been in the dungeon for a long time.

"Don't you want to go home?" Sally asked him one day. "Or don't you want to see your children?"

"Where is your Papa?" the man changed the subject. "Do you live with him?"

Oliver sighed, "Yes, I live with my Papa and Mama. I have a brother and sister also. We live in the house up there," he pointed upwards. "Sally's aunt is the one who cooks the food in our house."

"She makes good things, like the ones we bring for you," Sally added.

"What about your father?"

Sally pouted, "Aunt Anne told me that my Papa and Mama are in heaven. They went to live there, and one day I will see them again."

"Children, remember it's very important that you never tell anyone where I am or that you've seen me. Is that clear?'

"You already told us that," Oliver said, "Why don't you want to go home to your family?"

The man looked really sad. "I had a very beautiful wife and son, but they both died. I got sick and had to come down here so that no one can hurt me."

"But you are in chains," Sally rattled the chains. "Who takes them off you?"

"No one, but like I said, don't tell anyone that I am in here."

The children nodded.

"Now you need to run along because your parents and your aunt might be looking for you."

"Can we come and see you tomorrow?" Sally asked. She always requested permission to return the next day, and whenever they did, she had something for him to eat.

"Yes, I would like that very much."

◠

"Sally, there's something going on, and I am getting worried," Anne looked at her niece when they were in their home, "Recently you have started disappearing from the kitchen, and I don't know where you go to. I hope you're not causing any trouble or spoiling anything in the manor. If Mrs. Winchester finds you, she will send us away, and then we won't have anywhere else to live."

Sally really wanted to tell her aunt about the man in the dungeon, but Oliver had sworn her to secrecy. He was her best friend, and she never wanted to hurt him or get him into trouble.

"Well? Where have you been disappearing to?"

Sally swallowed knowing that she would have to lie to her aunt. "Playing."

"Where?"

"Outside"

"With the other children?" Anne's tone was impatient.

Sally gasped audibly. "No," she croaked, "With the cat."

Anne gave her a long look then sighed, shaking her head, "Just make sure you don't go causing trouble for anyone. I don't want you roaming all over the house, because Mrs. Winchester will be very upset if she catches you."

"I'm sorry."

"Stop saying that and come here." Anne held her hands out and Sally didn't hesitate. Much as her aunt was strict and often chastised her, Sally also knew that she was loved. "I brought you a cream tart."

"You did?" Sally's eyes lit up, and Anne laughed. She loved this little girl, her brother's daughter, and many times her heart wept with the knowledge that her brother wasn't around to see his daughter growing. "Aunt Anne, you look sad."

"No," Anne said with a forced laugh. "Hand me my coat so I can give you the cream tart before it gets all mashed up."

◞

"One day you'll pay for this meanness to me," Oliver sobbed as his brother hit him repeatedly while Maeve cheered on. They had come into his room and found him just as he was waking up, and he hadn't been able to hide in the passageway like he usually did.

"Who'll make me pay, you insolent boy?" Kent slapped him hard, and he fell across the bed. Just as he was about to continue striking Oliver with hard fists, the door opened, and Anne entered the room.

"What do you think you're doing, Kent?" she asked him.

"Nothing," he moved toward the door.

"Then why is Oliver crying?"

"He's just a big cry baby," Maeve teased, then blushed when Anne turned her eyes on her.

"This is your little brother, and you should be protecting him. Instead, here you are beating him up. What's wrong with the two of you? Have you no shame and mercy?"

"Don't talk to us like that," Kent glared at her, "You're only a servant in this house, and you should know your place, or else I will tell my mother that you insulted me. Then she will kick you out of this house. Come on Maeve, let's go." At the door he turned and pointed at Oliver, "And you, this isn't over."

Anne waited until they had left before she turned to the crying boy. "Come with me, Oliver." She held out her hand and he rose from the bed. He felt pain all over and wiped his eyes. "I'm sorry they hurt you."

"I'm sorry they hurt you."

"Why do they hate me so much?" Oliver asked in a small voice. "They find any reason to beat me up."

"And have you ever told your parents whatever is going on?" Oliver nodded, "Didn't they warn them?"

"Father says we should settle matters on our own, and as for mother," He frowned. "She doesn't care what those two do to me."

"That's not right," Anne muttered, as she led the boy down the stairs and to the kitchen. "Sit under that table. My niece Sally is there."

Oliver slipped under the table, and Sally took his hand. The two children grinned at each other, hiding their secret. Aunt Anne had no idea that they had been playing together for many months. He quickly told her about Aunt Anne saving him from his brother and sister.

"I'm sorry they hurt you," Sally said. "When I grow up and become big like Aunt Anne, I will beat up Kent and Maeve, and they will never hurt you again." Her voice and face were fierce, and somehow Oliver felt comforted.

"When we grow big, we'll run away from here and go live far away where they can't find us. And we'll take the man in the dungeon with us, "Oliver said.

"Which man?" Anne had caught just a bit of the conversation. She knelt down and pushed two plates of food towards the children. "What are you two talking about?"

"The man in the stable," Sally said hastily, casting a glance at Oliver. "Oliver says he will teach him how to ride a horse," Sally grimaced, hating that she was lying to her beloved aunt, but knowing that she had to protect Oliver and the man in the dungeon. Oliver's eyes were on the feast laid out before him, and he fell upon the food like a starving man. In no time, the mashed potatoes, beef gravy, and peas were gone, and his eyes turned longingly towards Sally's plate.

"You can have mine too," she pushed the half-eaten plate towards him.

"What about you?"

"Aunt Anne will give me a pie when we go home."

"Thank you." Sally watched as Oliver devoured her portion too.

"Where is Tubby?"

"I think she went," he looked around, "To see our friend.

"We have to be very careful to never let anyone know that he's there," Sally said. "He made us promise."

"I know, but it's really hard keeping all this to myself."

Sally snorted, "Then don't talk to anyone, so you won't have to tell them anything."

Replete, the two children curled up on the rag and slept. At some point Tubby crawled between them, and it was quite late before Oliver woke up. He found himself alone in the kitchen, but Tubby lay close by. There were no candles in the kitchen, but the fire in the grate was still burning merrily. He knew that it would burn until morning. He saw a covered plate under the table and found more food, which he devoured. Sally's aunt must have left it for him to eat when he woke up. As he feasted on more mashed potatoes, green peas, and gravy, he listened for any sounds in the house. All was quiet, and he wondered if his brother and sister had tried to find him again.

Once he'd eaten, he remembered the man in the dungeon. They hadn't visited him that day because of what had happened with Kent and Maeve.

Crawling out of his new hiding place, Oliver looked around to see if there was any more food that he could steal. Usually it was Sally who brought the food they would take to their friend. He noticed the large wooden barrel near the door. He knew that Sally's aunt used it to put in whatever scraps of food were intended for the pigs, and he wished he had better light. Using the plate that he'd finished eating from, he scooped whatever was in the pot, praying that it would be edible. Tubby was running in circles around him.

"Tubby, we have to go to the man and bring him food." Oliver knew that there was another way into the dungeon, but he didn't want to get lost. Once he was sure everyone was in bed, he crept up to his bedroom and slipped under the bed.

"I didn't think you would come today." The man ate hungrily, not caring what was on the plate that Oliver had given him.

"I'm sorry," Oliver said. He wished he could share his troubles with his friend but decided not to. Besides, it wasn't as if the man could help him. But for some reason just being with the prisoner gave him some measure of comfort. There was a small fire burning in the corner of the cell, which Oliver knew someone had obviously lit.

"Why is the floor wet today?" Oliver looked around to see if there was a crack in the wall. "It hasn't rained so where did the water come from?"

"You children ask too many questions but to answer you, the people who have put me here come in to wash me once a week. That's why there's water on the floor today but don't worry, by tomorrow it will have dried up and the floor won't be so wet."

"But you must be cold all the time."

"Don't worry about me. I have the horse blanket that you and your friend brought me, and the fire also helps a lot."

$$\sim$$

A few days later, when Sally and Oliver came in to visit their friend in the dungeon, they found him lying on the floor. He was breathing with difficulty and coughing.

"He's really sick," Sally said with a tremor in her voice. "I don't like seeing him so sick."

"Mister," Oliver tried to shake the man, but he only rumbled, his eyes closed. "What are we going to do?"

"This place is so cold, and there's no fire today," Sally walked around the cell. "We should light a fire for him and then he will be warm."

"But we don't have anything with us. There's no wood in here."

"Oliver, can we go down the tunnels to see if we can find wood or something to light a fire with?"

Being in agreement, they left the cell and went down the tunnel. They hadn't gone far when they heard voices. "Hide," Oliver told Sally and they slipped into a small cell and lay low. Footsteps sounded past them and they listened. It sounded like there were two people.

"Briggs, I told you that this man is sick," one of them said. It was a male voice. "Look at how pathetic he looks. What if he dies?"

"We can't let him die, because there's so much at stake here. Maybe we should get him something like a mattress and blanket, and then ensure that there's enough wood for fire."

"The Madam said that we shouldn't give him any luxuries."

"Listen, it's better that we get him something more to keep him warm and alive. You know what will happen if he dies."

"Let's go and see what we can do."

The children waited for the men to leave before crawling out of their hiding place. "Let's go back to the kitchen," Sally said. "They will definitely come back."

"The other day, I followed Tubby and found another way out of the dungeon, but it leads to the pantry. We have to be very careful because we don't want anyone to know that we come down here, or they will stop us."

"Who do you think those two men were?"

"I don't know, and I wouldn't like to find out, because they frightened me. Let's go, Sally."

Sally ran to the kitchen and got under the table as usual, Oliver quickly following her.

"You two, what are you doing down there?" Pauline came and bent down, a frown on her face. "I thought you were playing outside. Why have you run into the kitchen? Don't you know that Mrs. Winchester will be so upset if she comes in and finds you vagabonds running loose in her kitchen? Come out right now," she hissed, and the children quickly slid from under the table. "Now, I know you're hungry, but it's not yet time for lunch. Run along now, and don't come in here again, or I'll box your ears."

Sally was trembling as she sat down behind a small bush at the back of the house. Pauline had no idea who she really was. Of course, in the days past the woman had found her skulking in the bushes and ignored her, probably thinking she was the child of one of the other servants. Sally didn't understand why her aunt never wanted anyone to know who she was, and she was getting tired of hiding under the table.

"Aunt Anne," she asked her later that evening when theywere back home. "Why can't I come out to play with the other children? I don't want to continue hiding under the table, and today Pauline found us and chased us out of the kitchen."

"Us? Who were you with?"

"Oliver, of course," Sally looked at her as if she'd asked a very strange question. "He hides with me every day, so his brother and sister won't beat him up."

"Sally, we've talked about this. I don't want Mrs. Winchester finding you and thinking that you're spoiling her things."

"But Aunt Anne, if I play outside with the other children then she won't find me. I will make sure that when they go home, I will hide in the stable until you come and get me. Please Aunt Anne."

Anne sighed, "Alright then, let's see how things go but please don't ever go to anyone's house. Play in the backyard and stay in the stable until I get you."

8

THE NARROW ESCAPE

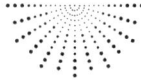

A nne tried to tug her chin away from Grant Winchester's large hand, but he held fast. He was taller and broader than she, and he had pinned her to the wall.

Though it was very early in the morning, his breath smelled foul, like stale whiskey and cigars. She nearly gagged.

"Let me go!" She tried to struggle but he only pressed himself closer.

"I've been watching for you and waiting," he said, trying to put his lips on hers, but she clamped hers shut. He pressed her chin and forced her mouth open, slipping his thick tongue in, and she brought her teeth down. He yelped, taking a step back.

His face was dark with anger, and he grabbed her neck with both hands, squeezing until she felt like she couldn't breathe. "You think you can escape from my hands," he hissed, an ugly look that frightened her on his face.

"Please," her small hands beat at his huge ones. "Don't defile me, please," she felt the tears, but she was getting weak. She couldn't imagine that she was going to be ravaged on the kitchen floor, with Sally being very close by.

Grant ripped her thin blouse, but before he could touch her, something hissed and flew at him.

~

Sally was dozing in her usual corner under the table when she became aware of a struggle somewhere in the kitchen. Peeking furtively, she saw the master of the house. He had pushed her aunt to the wall, and she was crying, trying to fight him off.

Sally wanted to help but she was small. Why had she insisted on asking her aunt for a birthday cake? Today was her sixth birthday, and because they didn't have an oven at home in their small cottage, her aunt had decided to come in very early before Pauline woke up. Whenever her aunt wanted to bake her a special cake or pie, they would come in very early before anyone else was up.

But now Oliver's father was hurting her aunt, and Sally felt very helpless, so she started crying, and then felt something slip past her. The next minute she heard a loud shriek and Tubby flew onto Mr. Winchester's head.

"Get off me!" He stumbled backwards and tried to get the cat off his head, but Tubby wouldn't let go.

"Get him, Tubby," Sally cheered on softly, and then once Mr. Winchester was on the other side of the kitchen, Sally ran to her aunt and pressed herself at her side. Both of them were trembling, and watched in horrified fascination as Mr. Winchester danced around the kitchen with Tubby covering

71

his face. The cat had its claws stuck in the man's thick neck, and he was roaring in pain.

When he got close to the large cauldron in the grate, the cat jumped on his back and he lost his footing. As Sally and Anne watched, Mr. Winchester stumbled forward, arms flailing, and then fell face first into the cauldron. That pot never had anything cold in it for it remained boiling the whole night. Anne always boiled bones for broth and stock overnight for use the next day, and today was no different. As soon as they had come into kitchen, she had added more firewood in the grate, and the pot was boiling furiously, steam rising up.

"Oh, no," Anne put her hands to her lips and looked down at her niece.

Mr. Winchester wriggled then pulled his head out and crashed to the ground, moaning in pain. "The devil got me," he was screaming, and Sally heard doors being slammed somewhere in the house.

"Let's go," Anne said. She grabbed Sally's hand and they fled from the house. They didn't stop running until they got to their small cottage. It was still dark, and Anne lit a candle with trembling hands.

"We have to get away from here," she muttered as she hastily threw their few belongings into an old canvas bag.

"Where are we going?" Sally asked in a trembling voice.

"Far, far away, Sally. We can no longer stay here because of Mr. Winchester," Anne said. "We don't have any money, but we can't stay here. She looked around, "I'm sorry that I couldn't bake you a cake, my love," she said. "But when we're settled, I'll buy or bake you one."

"Aunt Anne?"

"Yes, my love?"

"I picked this up from the floor," Sally held up a small purse. It was heavy with coins.

"It must have fallen out of Mr. Winchester's pocket."

"There's money so we can go away, I don't want to stay here because that bad man wanted to hurt you."

"Let's go then."

〜

Oliver didn't know what woke him up, and he lay there in the darkness, heart pounding. Ever since his brother had tried to strangle him, he no longer felt comfortable sleeping in his bed. He had taken to crawling under his bed just so he could get some sleep.

He blinked rapidly in the darkness to see if someone had entered his room. But Tubby lay beside him, so he knew he was safe. The cat was his guardian, alerting him of any danger.

"Tubby, did you hear that?" he could hear the cocks crowing and knew that it was nearly morning. Sally had told him that her aunt had promised to come in very early so she could bake her a birthday cake. He worried that something had happened to Sally or Aunt Anne. The two had been very kind to him and he felt closer to them than his own family.

Just last evening, Sally had whispered that Aunt Anne had promised to find a way for the locksmith to come and put a bolt on his door so he could lock it from the inside. In that way, he could stop his siblings from entering his room whenever they wanted to hurt him.

Crawling from under the bed he listened for any sounds.; Hearing none, he crept to the door and slowly opened it. Tubby shot ahead, and he ran after her until she got to the kitchen. That's when he heard another groan.

"Aunt Anne?" Heart pounding, Oliver entered further into the kitchen, but then stopped and stared at the figure on the ground. "Pa?" His father was lying on the kitchen floor. To his knowledge, his father never set foot in this part of the house.

"You evil child!" Grant Winchester screamed, and Oliver heard a gasp behind him. It was the other cook, the one who didn't like him. Sally had told him that Pauline was very unpleasant and liked to carry tales to his mother.

"Oliver, what did you do to your father?" Pauline screamed.

"I didn't do anything to him. I heard him crying out and came to check; then I found him lying on the floor and screaming."

"Little liar," Pauline hissed. "Wait until your mother comes and sees what you've done." Pauline began to scream, the sound hurting Oliver's ears. He moved toward the kitchen door that led into the backyard, knowing he had to get away. Pauline meant him evil and he wasn't going to wait around for it.

The kitchen was soon filled with people, and everyone was talking at once but the voice which stood out was Pauline's. "I found Oliver standing over his father with a hot pot." she was saying, "He was the one who poured the hot broth on Mr. Winchester, scalding his face."

"Where is that good-for-nothing spawn of the devil," Oliver heard his mother's voice. He crept out of the kitchen, but one of the stable boys saw him. "There he is!" He shouted as

Oliver darted out of the house and ran as fast as his little legs could carry him.

"Find him and bring him here. He is a criminal and must be dealt with before he murders us all in our beds," his mother shrieked.

Knowing that he couldn't run very far, Oliver remembered the old well he had discovered a few days before. It was old, and grass had grown all over it, so no one could tell it was there. He ran and didn't think about fear, because he knew if he was caught, things would end up badly for him. He didn't stop to think about snakes or scorpions as he slipped into the old well and clung to the thick creeper and jutting rocks. It didn't once occur to him that there could be dangerous creatures hiding in the thick foliage. All his thoughts were concentrated on hiding from those who were pursuing him. He could hear people running above ground, and he prayed that none of them would discover the old well or remember that it was there. His hands grew tired and he felt himself slipping.

"I'm dying today," he thought as he felt himself falling. It wasn't a great drop, but it jarred his teeth. He felt a blast of cold air, and he peered into what seemed to be a passage at the bottom of the well. He slipped through and realized this was another entrance into the dungeons, one that had been long-forgotten, judging from the cobwebs he had to fight through. He had no idea where he was going, but after stumbling in the darkness for a while, he found himself standing in front of the cell where his friend was.

The man was startled from his sleep, and his eyes widened when he saw Oliver. "What is going on, and why do you look like you're panting? Is someone chasing you?"

"Yes," Oliver said, looking around in fear, as if expecting someone to come at him.

"Come and sit with me for a while," he raised the blanket. "Those people brought me a mattress and blanket a few days ago, and it isn't as cold as it used to be. Stay here and when all is well out there, you can go back." But Oliver knew that he wouldn't be returning to the house ever again.

9

STRANGERS IN THE CITY

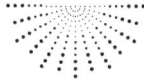

The next few days were really difficult for Anne and Sally as they sought a place to live in London. Even though their journey had been made in haste, the child had enjoyed the train ride from Bristol to London, gazing excitedly at the passing scenery and asking her aunt many questions. She didn't like seeing her aunt looking so sad, so she tried her best to cheer her up. The journey took them just a few hours, and Sally was too excited to sleep. She was disappointed when they got to their journey's end and Aunt Anne took her hand.

"Where are we going now?"

"We have to find a place to live because we're in London, and this is Paddington Station," Anne said. "Stay close to me so you don't get lost."

Sally had never seen so many people in one place at the same time, and her eyes glowed. Her hand was held fast in her aunt's, but that didn't stop her from dragging behind and almost being crushed by the people.

"Sally, don't lag behind," Anne hissed. "I don't want to lose you."

They followed the crowd to the outside of the station where hawkers yelled as they peddled their wares. Horse buggies stood parked at awkward angles as their drivers shouted for customers. Sally took all this in, her eyes wide and her smile broad. But as they moved away from the station, Sally started drooping. She stumbled and fell, scraping her knees.

"I'm so sorry," Anne brushed the dust from her frock and then picked her up. "Let's find an inn to stay at tonight, and then tomorrow we can find a place to live and a position for me to work at."

∼

Even though the small room in the inn was dingy and dark, in an odd way, Sally seemed happy that they were away from the place where the horrid man had wanted to hurt her aunt, but she missed Oliver and Tubby and found herself wiping tears away. They spent a single night in the inn and the next morning they were out as soon as it was light.

"I'm sorry that I had to drag you away from the only home you've known for a long time." Anne said as they walked down a busy street. She stopped in front of a small cake shop that had tables on the sidewalk, "Wait, why don't I buy you a small cake so we can celebrate your birthday?"

The mention of cake had Sally smiling, and before long they were tucking into a generous piece of cake which was covered in delicious thick cream.

"Do you like it?"

Sally could only nod because her mouth was full. The young girl knew that they had many problems and would face a lot of challenges ahead. But for now, she was glad to take the load off her feet and enjoy the delicious treat. It was soon gone, and she stared longingly at the counter where many more delicacies were well arranged like pretty flowers in a field.

Anne wished she could spare another penny to get her niece another piece of cake. The coins in Mr. Winchester's purse were nearly gone, and they still had to find somewhere to stay. She knew that she was lucky to have a charge who never whined or complained.

Sally was the kind of child who graciously received whatever she was given. Even when there was nothing to give, the child never complained or threw tantrums. Anne was proud of the way she was trying so hard not to ask for another piece of cake.

"Here," Sally and Anne looked up to see a beaming middle-aged man bearing down on them. He was short and very round, and Sally's young mind told her that he probably over-indulged in his own delicacies, but his smile was infectious, and she found herself smiling back at him. In his hand was a large saucer with big piece of cake on it.

"But we didn't order another cake," Anne could see Sally's fingers just itching to grab it and shovel it into her small mouth. "I'm sorry, but I don't have the money to pay for this extra piece. I thank you all the same."

"Don't you worry your head, little lady," he scratched his beard, "Today I happened to bake more than usual, and I could see that your pretty daughter hasn't quite had enough." He reached out his free hand and ruffled Sally's pigtails. "She is a very delightful child, and well-mannered, too. I think she deserves another piece of cake," he winked at Sally, "Or what do you think, little one?" Sally wanted to nod in agreement, her eyes fixed on the delicious-looking cake in the man's hand. But Aunt Anne scowled at her, so she looked down, her fingers twisting in her lap.

"Thank you, but no," Anne's voice was firm. She never accepted charity from anyone, because in her experience nothing came for free. "I can't pay for the piece of cake and wouldn't feel right about accepting it for free."

The man looked at her and then nodded, "Perchance are you looking for work? My wife and I run this place, but she is laid up for a week now."

"I'm sorry. Is she very ill?" Anne's concern was immediate and genuine. Now that she looked at the man closely, she could see that he looked rather harassed. "I hope she gets better soon."

The man laughed and shook his head. "Oh no, my dear wife isn't ill. The good Lord has blessed us with our sixth child, a boy this time, after five girls," he laughed and looked around him. The other tables were empty, and there were only two other customers inside the shop itself. "Why don't you accept this piece as a way to help me celebrate the birth of my son?"

"If you put it like that, thank you, because yesterday was Sally's birthday ," Anne pushed the cake toward Sally, who fell upon it like she was starving. "Slow down child, or you will choke."

"I'll bring you some lemonade. Then we can talk about you helping me out for a few days until my wife returns."

〜

Hans Schroeder was a Belgian of German descent, whose grandfather Sebastian Schroeder came to London after all his family was killed during the Napoleonic wars. At the time, he was just ten years old and had stowed away on a trawler. Once in London, young Sebastian had roamed the streets and ended up working for a man who owned a tavern. The man's wife loved to bake, and she was had taught Sebastian Hans to produce delicacies that had customers coming back for more. As the young boy grew, so did his love for baking, and when he was of age, his master gave him his freedom. He started his own bakery and café.

"This little café has been passed down from my grandfather to my father and now me. Now I can pass it to my son when he comes of age," Hans beamed at Sally and Anne as he showed them where they would sleep. "I'm afraid that this is just the store where we keep the sacks of flour and our other supplies. At least there are no rats because we have a cat that takes care of that problem." He looked around. "I don't see her right now, but she'll be around soon. Maybe my wife will be agreeable to you staying on, and then we can find you a small room to rent."

"Thank you, Mr. Hans," Anne said and looked at Sally. They couldn't believe their good fortune, for Anne had been very worried about where they would sleep that night.

Life settled down, and even though Anne wasn't making much money at the job, they at least had something to eat and a clean place to sleep. Mr. Hans had even gone so far as to bring them a thin mattress and two thick blankets. In the evenings, when Mr. Hans closed the shop, he made sure to give Anne and Sally the leftovers and broken pastries which wouldn't be sold the next day. Sally became friends with the cat, which reminded her of Tubby. Each time she played with the cat, she thought about Oliver and Tubby and was sad for a while, but Helen of Troy, as Mr. Hans had named his cat, would get up to her funny theatrics which would soon have Sally giggling happily once again.

"We can't eat all this," Anne told Sally during their second week at the shop. "Let's sell whatever we can spare so we can buy some good food and maybe even save a little money."

"But this is good food, Aunt Anne."

"Only you would think that, little Sally, seeing as how much you love cake and pastries." Anne stroked her hair. "But we can't live on cakes, cookies, and doughnuts. Don't you miss a good plate of beans and rice, or a rich shepherd's pie with steaming vegetables?"

"I miss them, Aunt Anne." Sally licked her small lips as she remembered the delicious food her aunt used to cook at Oliver's house.

"That's why we have to sell what Mr. Hans gives us so we can buy proper food."

$$\approx$$

For the next three months, as Mrs. Hans was away from the bakery, Sally and Anne prospered. Anne would wake up very early and leave Sally still sleeping with the cat cuddled up close to her. She would open the bakery and stir the old wood stove back to life, and then place the day's baking into the oven. By the time Mr. Hans appeared at around seven o'clock, a good portion of the baking had been done, and all that was left was to clean the cafe and set out the tables on the pavement to get ready for their first customers. These were usually young men and women on their way to work in the offices and thread factory down the road.

"You seem to have the hang of the business," Mr. Hans told her one morning when he came in. "For a while now, I've been thinking about opening a second bakery and café, and I was even looking at a property the other day. When my wife returns to work, we will definitely expand this small business," he smiled. "Good times lie ahead of you, Miss Cotton. I know that we will build Hans and Son's Bakery into a large business. We shall all prosper, just you wait and see."

That dream died before it could become a reality. Things changed when Mrs. Lucille Hans returned to the bakery. She took one look at Anne, frowned, and proceeded to make the day a really trying one for her. Lucille Hans was a tall, thin woman with a constant frown on her face and bitter grey eyes. What Anne didn't know was that the woman felt quite threatened by her youthful appearance. Throughout that day when Lucille wasn't shouting at her for one thing or the other, Anne noticed her giving her strange looks that frightened her.

"I don't think Mrs. Hans likes us," Sally said pensively that evening, "She was shouting at you all the time."

"You're just imagining things, child," Anne said with a small laugh. "Mrs. Hans has just had a baby, and it must be hard for her. Things will get better, you'll see."

Over the next few days, things didn't get any better; if anything, they got worse. Gone were the leftovers that Mr. Hans used to give them. Anne and Sally both had to work very hard cleaning the café and washing dishes. One evening Mr. Hans had to leave early to look at the property he'd been thinking of acquiring, leaving his wife to lock up. She deliberately locked up the store where Sally and Anne slept and went home with the key, leaving them with nowhere to sleep that night.

Anne tried to bust the lock but it was well fitted, and so she pushed the large outside table they used for kneading dough against the wall and that night they huddled under it. Anne couldn't sleep because she had to protect Sally, who didn't once complain. She played with Helen of Troy until very late, and then they ate crumbs scraped off the large table because the little money they had was locked up in the store and Aunt Anne couldn't buy them any food.

"Why are we sleeping outside today, Aunt Anne?" Sally asked sleepily, quite exhausted from not only playing with Helen of Troy but also after scrubbing tables till her small hands were raw with burst blisters.

"Sh! Don't talk so loudly," Anne said as she drew her niece closer. At least they had some old jute flour sacks to cover themselves with. Her prayer was that no one would find them there and attack them.

Dawn was breaking when Anne started dozing off, only to be awakened by loud footsteps.

"What is going on here?" Anne and Sally were startled when they heard Mr. Hans's loud voice over their heads. He bent down to peer at them and then straightened himself. "Why did you sleep outside when I gave you the store?"

Not willing to look like she was reporting his wife, Anne looked down. Mr. Hans walked to the small store and turned the handle. It was locked. His wife came up then.

"Why did you lock the store?"

"Don't we always lock it?" She cast a malicious glare towards Anne and Sally. "That's where we store our supplies, and if we leave it open the riffraff might steal from us."

"I thought I told you that Miss Cotton and her daughter sleep in the store till they can find somewhere else to sleep."

"What I recall is you telling me that she was hired temporarily. You said that as soon as I came back to the store you would send her away. Why then is she still here? This is the fourth month that she has been here, and it doesn't look like she is leaving soon. Or is she your mistress and this one is your child? Tell me the truth, Hans! Is Anne your mistress?"

"Woman, don't talk nonsense," Hans growled, "Miss Cotton needed work so she could take care of her child. What's more, we had talked about opening the second bakery and you were quite agreeable. What's gotten into you?"

"At the time you mentioned Miss Cotton, I thought she was an older woman who wouldn't give us any trouble."

"Miss Cotton hasn't given us any trouble, and if anything, business has been picking up very well since she came here. That's why we'reeven able to think about opening a second bakery."

"I want her gone from here today," Mrs. Hans hissed at her husband.

"Miss Cotton is going nowhere," and the two glared at each other like they would rip each other apart.

When Anne realized the couple was about to get into a real fight, she stepped forward, "Mr. Hans, thank you for your kindness, but I don't want to cause any trouble between the two of you when you've been so kind to us. Sally and I will go, but please just allow me to pick up our few belongings from the store."

"Good," Mrs. Hans said as tossed the keys at her husband and stomped into the shop, but Mr. Hans looked troubled.

"You don't have to leave. My wife will come around. She's a good woman."

Anne shook her head, "You need to have peace in your home and at your place of business, sir. Please, just allow us to leave."

"Where will you go?" Anne shrugged. "I know! Please go to Euston Street, house number thirty-one. My sister is the housekeeper there. Tell her I sent you, and she will take care of you." He pressed some money into her hands and then opened the store for them to pick up their belongings. Once Anne and Sally were ready to leave, Mr. Hans hurried to join his wife in the shop.

10

FOR WORSE

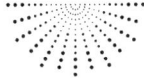

During the next few years, Sally found herself working very hard alongside her aunt. While Aunt Anne washed and cleaned houses for the middle-income clients, Sally spent the time in sole charge of their children. She was growing up very fast and Anne was really worried because the child was so beautiful. Men had started looking at her in a funny way. Protecting Sally was all Anne thought about every day, and she worked hard so they could buy their own house somewhere in the country.

While London was a good place to work, it was also a town full of vices that turned the stomachs of decent folk. Getting Sally to the countryside was the best thing to do, because by the time she became a teenager, men would be beating down their door. What Anne didn't realise was that, because she shared similar features with her niece, she too was an object of many a man's appraisal. One man had even been heard to call them the Golden Sisters.

Aunt Anne cleaned for five different families, allocating a day of the week for each. On Mondays it was Mrs. Shear, Tuesdays belonged to Mrs. Queen, Wednesdays were taken by Mrs. Brown, while Thursday and Friday belonged to Mrs. Carry and Mrs. Winters respectively. It was funny that all five women had two children each, all much younger than Sally, who had turned nine with much aplomb. Now that they had a steady income, Aunt Anne was able to buy her a cake from Mr. Hans's shop.

Mr. Hans still had the same welcoming smile on his face, but he'd lost his wife Lucille the year before when she was giving birth. She brought forth another son, but he died just two days after his mother. Mr. Hans then married the governess who was taking care of his children. Though the news made Sally and Anne sad, they could never forget how Mrs. Lucille Hans had ill-treated them.

"Sally," her aunt told her on the night of her ninth birthday, after they had eaten the cake and even had some left over. "Never be bad to people or mistreat them just because you can do so. It's not right, and you should always seek to be kind to people. Do you understand?"

"Yes, Aunt Anne," Sally said. "I was sad to hear that Mrs. Lucille died."

"Yes, child, it's a very sad thing that her children will grow up without their mother. I know it hasn't been easy for you all these years without your parents. They would be very proud of the good girl you've grown up to be."

"But I have you, Aunt Anne, and I'm not sad all the time."

"You also brought life back into my life, Sally, and I love you very much. Now we have to sleep because we need to get up early and go to work tomorrow as usual. You know how much work Mrs. Winters likes to give us, even though she pays us something extra each day."

Sally nodded and prepared for bed, thinking about all the work they did during the week. She never complained, because every Saturday her aunt took her on a ride in one of the horse buggies around London. On Sundays, they would go to church and then spend the rest of the day at Hyde Park. Sally's favourite pastime on Sundays was walking along the Serpentine River and crossing the bridge as they watched wealthy people riding their horses, or lovers strolling hand in hand along the different pathways lined with flowers, pretty shrubs and trees forming shade in summer.

"Will we go to the park again this Sunday, Aunt Anne?" Sally asked sleepily.

"Of course, my dear," Anne tucked her niece in. "The only time we don't go to the park is when it's raining or snowing. Since the weather is still warm, we shall certainly visit again."

"Aunt Anne, Mrs. Winters asked me where your husband is."

Anne started, glad that the small candle wasn't bright enough for her face to be clear to her inquisitive niece. "What did you tell her?"

Sally shrugged, "I told her to ask you herself." Sally sat up. "Aunt Anne, do you have a husband?"

"Why are you asking me so many questions today, dear child?"

"If you had a husband then you would have children, and I could play with them. I like children, but the people we work for don't allow us to bring the children to our home. Will you get married and have children?"

"One day," Anne said sadly, not wishing to think about her great loss.

"You look sad. I'm sorry to ask so many questions." Sally slipped back under the blankets. "Are you angry with me for asking you questions?"

"Sally, I could never be angry with you! And thank you for telling Mrs. Winters to talk to me about my husband. If anyone asks you anything, just tell them to speak to me."

"I like playing with children," Sally murmured sleepily as she struggled to keep her eyes open. "The mothers are also nice."

Sally's favourite was the family they cleaned and washed for on Wednesdays. Mrs. Brown was a lovely woman who never stopped smiling. She always had something for Anne and Sally to take home with them when they were done with their work. She even gave them clothes and other pretty trinkets.

It wasn't that the families didn't have other household servants. They needed Aunt Anne to do the laundry and thorough cleaning of the common areas of their homes. Their usual servants would do the other tasks, like cooking and taking care of the children, as well as cleaning the private bedchambers where Anne and Sally weren't allowed to venture.

Anne felt that they had been lucky because although Mr. Han's sister, Imogene, was a very unfriendly woman, she'd given them the chance to work. Imogene knew the owners of many households, and she was the one who had arranged for Anne to work for the five families. It was really hard work, and even though the families paid slightly better wages than what Mr. Hans used to pay Aunt Anne, Imogene demanded half of it.

≈

Sally finally fell asleep, much to Anne's relief. The child's questions had stirred up painful memories for her, and she couldn't stop them from flooding her mind.

From the time she'd lost her husband several years ago and gone to live with her brother and mean sister-in-law, Anne's goal had been to save whatever money she made. Her greatest desire was that she would one day have her own little cottage in the country somewhere. Then her brother and sister-in-law perished in the fire, and their lives had taken a drastic turn. Coming to London was supposed to have enabled her to achieve her dream faster, but no matter how hard she worked and tried to save, the expenses were just too great. Taking care of herself and Sally was no mean feat, and she worried that she would never achieve her dream.

She still missed Ernest, even though he'd never become her husband in the real sense of the word. Thinking about getting married to someone else was also too painful because she couldn't imagine falling in love again and then losing her husband. It would just kill her. So, she took comfort in her life with Sally and put all thoughts of romantic nonsense behind her.

In any case, she didn't think anyone would want a thirty-two-year-old woman as a wife when there were so many pretty young women around. She was destined to be a spinster, and all she could look forward to was bringing Sally up, and then when she was grown, finding her a good husband. The only children Anne hoped to hold on her knees were her grandchildren from Sally.

"We'll never get anywhere at this rate," Sally heard her aunt talking to herself in the deep of the night a few months later. They had a small room in a townhouse in Everton, Whitechapel, and the landlady, though quite strict, was also very fair. She had converted her old house into small units of single rooms on the ground floor and doubles on the first floor. Anne and Sally liked most about the house was the fact that there were no men living in the building. Mrs. Crowe, who was a childless widow herself, only rented her rooms to single women and widows with one or two children at most. Her one rule was that none of her tenants would bring any men into her building. According to a neighbour, once a tenant's sons reached the age of fifteen, Mrs. Crowe would end the tenancy agreement between them and ask the family to find other quarters. No one understood why she was so against having males in her building, and no one was brave enough to ask the question that was in their minds.

"Aunt Anne, is everything alright?" Sally asked.

"Go to sleep child," Anne said in her soft voice. "It's nothing that should worry you."

Sally knew that her aunt was really worried about their livelihood. Whatever money she made was just enough to cover their rent, and there was usually very little left for anything else.

"I have to find a way of getting some money," Sally thought. "Then Aunt Anne will be happy." The child knew that her aunt had sacrificed a lot by keeping her. She could just as well have dumped her at an orphanage or even disappeared, but Aunt Anne had made a promise to her one day when she found Sally crying.

"What's wrong child?"

"Aunt Anne, will you also go away and leave me like my Pa and Ma?"

"Oh Sally," Anne gathered her in her arms and held her close, "Whatever gave you that horrible idea?"

"I heard Mrs. Crowe speaking to Mrs. Grey that I'm holding you back. Mrs. Crowe said that she would like you to go and become her widowed brother's wife so you can take care of his two children. But she said I am holding you back because her brother will never accept a woman who has a child tagging along."

"Sally, I would never give you up just to go and take care of another man's children," Anne said in a tight voice.

"But I'm not even your child." Sally sniffed and wiped her runny nose on the back of her hand. "I am not your child," she repeated.

"Don't ever say that," Anne scolded in a mild voice. "You are my child and if a man ever wants to marry me, he will have to accept you as well."

Even though Sally was appeased for the moment, she still carried a deep fear within her heart that she was a burden to her aunt. If Aunt Anne really wanted to go and be Mrs. Crowe's brother's wife, she was standing in her way.

If only Oliver was here, the young girl thought. He would help her think of what to do. She wondered if she could find a way to go back to the manor. She could hide in the dungeon with the stranger who lived there, and Oliver would bring them food. Then when she was all grown up, she could work in the house. Maybe she and Oliver would get married and move away, taking the man in the dungeon with them, and of course, Tubby.

As she thought about working for Oliver's mother, she shuddered. She was afraid Mr. Winchester would press himself on her the way he had tried to do to Aunt Anne. Instead, she would ask Oliver if she could live in the dungeon and then find work in another household.

"Sally?" Anne whispered, "Are you asleep?"

"No."

"Did you read your books today?"

"Yes, Aunt Anne."

"Good, and do you have any questions for me?"

"No."

"All right then go to sleep."

"Yes, Aunt Anne."

But sleep was a long time in coming, and Sally listened as her aunt talked to herself for a long time.

$\sim$

For Oliver, the three years after he escaped from home were the hardest he'd ever experienced. Living in the forest and evading capture like a hunted animal was exhausting. Sometimes he felt that he should just give in and go back home, but then he would remember the man in the dungeon who needed him, and he would continue the cat and mouse game with his pursuers.

Twice in those three years, he came close to being captured. The first time it was Romani Gypsies who had saved his life. That was just about a month after he'd run away from home and hidden in the dungeon for days. Hunger had brought him out to the surface again, and he decided that hanging around the house would only lead to trouble. He found his way to the forest, keeping Tubby with him.

Being only ten at the time, he had no idea of how he would survive all alone, but he'd followed Tubby as she darted in and out of bushes, unaware that one of the stable boys had seen him and reported the fact to his parents. After running around the forest for a while, he was tired and decided to take a rest at the foot of a tree. Tubby kept nudging him, but his legs were shaking due to hunger, as he hadn't eaten the whole day.

He began to doze and thought he heard flutes being played. The sound was soft and soothing and lulled him to sleep. What the boy didn't realise was that he'd strayed into a Romani camp, or rather at the edge of one. Three Romani boys were trying to learn how to play their flutes when they became aware that there was a stranger in their midst, and that was when three burly men came crashing through the woods and the boys' screams alerted their parents of danger.

Oliver woke up to loud voices, and he crawled into a bush and stared at the colourfully dressed people arguing with three men dressed in regular clothes. He identified one man from the latter group as a stable boy on his parents' estate, and he knew that they had come in pursuit of him. Knowing that if they captured him, he would be in a lot of trouble, Oliver crawled through the thick foliage on the ground and ended up right under one of the caravans. Tubby never left his side, and when he looked up, he saw a strange-looking woman peering down at him. She smiled when she saw the cat circling his legs, and she beckoned to him. The aroma of roasting meat enticed him to follow her, and he soon found himself inside her caravan. There were a lot of odd-looking objects on the walls of her small living space, and it was the first time that he saw a crystal ball, which fascinated him.

"What is that?" He asked the woman, pointing at the spherical object. It seemed to be clear and then would suddenly mist up. The woman responded in a language he didn't understand, and he shrugged. She made motions for him to sit on the floor and she sat across from him, crossing her legs. Even though he should have been frightened of her strange appearance, there was something about her that made the young boy know that she would never hurt him.

She produced a plate of roast meat, and he wondered where it had come from. Too hungry to continue questioning the hand that was offering him food, he fell upon the meat, which was tender and succulent, feeding Tubby as he ate. Once he was replete, he felt sleepy and curled up on the floor, Tubby next to him, and fell asleep.

He woke up hours later and realised that the caravan was in motion. A man had joined the woman, and they sat there staring at him. "Who are you?" the man asked him, and Oliver was surprised to hear him speak good English.

"My name is Oliver and I-" He didn't want to let the man know that he was running away from home. They might take him back and hand him over to his mother. He could just imagine the kind of torture he would undergo at the hands of Maeve and Kent, not to mention their mother. "I want to go home," he said in a trembling voice, hoping his hosts would put him down by the wayside.

"It is night-time. Sleep, and in the morning, we will let you out."

Oliver stayed with the Romani community for nearly a month, during which time he discovered that they hadn't left Bristol at all. What they had done was move to a different part of the vast forest after clashing with the three men who had been pursuing him. The man he'd met on his first day with the Gypsies had told him that his name was Manfrid and the woman was Tillie. They became his good friends, even though the woman could barely speak English.

"We are headed to London for the winter," Manfrid told him one Friday afternoon. "Do you want to come with us? You know that we need young boys like you to help around the camp and with the various tasks that we do."

As much as he was tempted to go with his new family, Oliver felt that he would be abandoning the man in the dungeon. As it was, he hadn't been to see him for a full month, and he wondered how he was faring.

"I wish I could go with you, but I need to go back home," he said.

The next day, when the community broke camp, they left Oliver behind. He wiped the tears away from his eyes as he watched the colourful caravans driving away. Some of the children he'd made friends with waved at him, and he raised his hand in acknowledgement. He didn't know if he would ever see his good friends again.

As he turned to retrace his steps to the manor, he felt that he had matured in the month that he'd lived among the Gypsies. Tillie was a fortune teller, and he would watch as people came in to consult with her. Not all of them were from her community, and during those times when regular folk came to see her, Oliver would hide behind a curtain for fear of being recognized by any of them. Manfrid, who was a metal smith, had taught him how to tinker with metals and forge small utensils. Though he was sad to see them go, the young boy knew it was for the best.

"We may return in the spring to till the land," Manfrid told him as he gave him a change of clothing and a few shillings. Oliver was glad that his friend had given him dull clothes, not colourful ones like they wore. The last thing he wanted was to draw any attention to himself as he continued to live near the manor.

∼

The next time Oliver was nearly captured again by the stable boy from the manor, it was Tubby who saved him. It was early evening, and he'd slipped into the dungeon to visit his friend. That was a couple of days after he had left the Gypsies, and he was bringing his friend something to eat.

"You've been gone a while," the man said when he appeared in the cell, Tubby immediately going over to him. "I thought you had decided to never return."

"No, I had to go away for a while because there was some trouble."

"What happened?"

"My father got hurt and Pauline, the bad maid, told everyone that I was the one who hurt him."

"What do you mean by hurt?"

"I entered the kitchen in the morning and found my father on the floor. His face was peeling horribly like someone had poured hot broth on him. Then the maid came and found him crying and said it was me who had done it." Oliver bit his lower lip.

"Well, did you?"

"Did I what?"

"Did you burn your father?"

"No," the boy looked so horrified that the man chuckled softly. "I found him rolling on the floor and moaning. I don't know who burned him."

After a brief visit, Oliver got up to leave. He climbed out of the old well and had taken a few steps when he felt someone clap a strong hand on his shoulder. Startled, he cried out and tried to shake himself free.

"Got you," the stable boy said. "Now I will get the reward that is on your head." As he tried to drag Oliver away, Tubby jumped on the stable boy's head and began scratching him. Oliver took off for the forest, knowing that Tubby would eventually find him. After walking for a while, he came across an old hut which he guessed belonged to some wood cutters. It looked abandoned, and he stood there wondering whether to open the door and go in or not. His fear was finding some wild creature inside that would attack him, but Tubby came and walked right past him and stood scratching herself on the door, so he guessed that the place was safe.

"Thank you for saving me yet again," Oliver said. "I have to be really careful because those people will never stop looking for me."

Now, three years later, he still lived like a vagabond, roaming through the forest in search of food. The only time he felt at peace was when the Gypsies returned and he could be a part of their community, but they never stayed more than a few months at most and even though each time Manfrid begged him to go with them, Oliver could not abandon his friend in the dungeon.

He had learned how to stay out of the way of anyone who looked suspicious, even though he often sneaked back into the Manor to steal food and other items.

11

COMING OF AGE

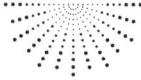

W e have to finish the washing early, child," Anne told Sally, "It looks like it will rain later in the afternoon. I don't want us getting caught up in the rain and then having to go home late. I don't like us walking in the dark because it's not safe."

"Yes, Aunt Anne," Sally said, scrubbing the clothes she had in her wooden barrel. It was her twelfth birthday today, and she was sad because it would probably pass without any cake. Aunt Anne had probably forgotten all about her birthday, and even so, they didn't have any money to buy a piece of cake. Mrs. Crowe had raised the rent she charged them to almost double what they used to pay, and Aunt Anne had started talking of them finding another place to live.

Sally liked living in Mrs. Crowe's house because it was clean and not too far from the houses where they worked, but with the increase in rent, they had to go without many things because they had to work on Saturdays as well. By Sunday, Aunt Anne was too tired to go to the park as they had done before.

Sally wiped her tears with the back of her hand. There would be no celebrating her birthday today, and that was one of the only things she looked forward to in her simple life each year. It was times like this that she thought about the small bakery owned by Mr. Hans with much longing. She knew that if she could only find her way there, he would give her a cake because he'd been doing so for the past few years after he found out that her birthday was the day before his only son's. After his wife had died and he married the children's governess, she went on to give him three daughters in the short space of three years, so he still had only one son. Mr. Hans would definitely give her a cake, but Sally hated asking her aunt to go out of her way to please her. She didn't want to agitate the woman who had taken care of her for so long, and knowing that she was the reason her aunt wasn't married made it even harder for her to ask for anything extra.

They got off work later that day, and it was getting dark and had started drizzling.

"Sally, we have to hurry home. "Anne grabbed her hand and hurried her. "It's not safe to be outside this late," she said, and Sally nodded.

She'd overheard Mrs. Crowe and Mrs. Grey talking about the young women who had been murdered by a man everyone was calling Jack the Ripper. Apparently, the man targeted young women found alone at night on the streets of White Chapel. No one had any idea of who he might be, because he never struck at the same place twice. The policemen were baffled, and no one knew what to do. But everyone,especially young women,were terrified, and they had been warned to never venture outside once it got dark.

They had turned into the alley that was just a few feet away from Mrs. Crowe's house when a man appeared out of nowhere. He was tall and thin, and even though Sally couldn't make out his face, there was something ominous about his presence. He seemed to have been waiting for them, and Aunt Anne pushed Sally behind her.

"Sally, run," Anne said in a frightened voice as the man approached them. This was the part of the alley that was dark and poorly lit, and there weren't any people walking around because it was drizzling. Sally held onto her aunt's hand and started crying, refusing to leave her. She was really frightened.

"Sally, run to the church and hide there," Anne said.

"No," the child clung to her aunt's dress even as the man approached and struck Anne hard, so she fell and hit her head on the pavement. He expected Sally to run away but she stood her ground and started screaming with all her might. The man grabbed Anne and started dragging her on the ground.

"Mrs. Crowe, this bad man has killed Aunt Anne. Mrs. Crowe, won't you help us?"

Suddenly Sally heard footsteps running toward them, and the man cursed, then dropped the unconscious Anne and fled.

"Child, what's wrong?" A man who Sally recognized as Old Peter the cobbler was standing over her. The dim streetlight cast shadows, and Sally was terrified that the horrible man would return.

"That man hit Aunt Anne," she was kneeling beside the still figure. "Aunt Anne is dead," she cried.

"No, she is only unconscious. Come; let me take you to the house where Mrs. Crowe will take care of you, and then I will come back and carry your aunt."

"No, I won't leave my aunt," Sally sobbed and to her relief she saw the front door of their house opening. "Mrs. Crowe," she screamed. A few of the other tenants from their house came running and they all helped carry Anne into the house, where they laid her on the bed.

"She doesn't have any visible wounds," Mrs. Crowe announced after examining her from top to bottom. "I don't see any blood or open wounds. This young woman was really lucky," she looked at Sally. "This would not have happened if your aunt had agreed to go to the countryside as my brother's wife, but she said she could not leave you behind." Her tone was accusatory. "I'm sure that was Jack the Ripper, and this time you were lucky. What about the next time, when Mr. Peter can't come to your rescue?"

Sally wept as she watched over her aunt for the next two days. This was all her fault. If she hadn't been in her aunt's life, she would now be married and safe in a countryside cottage with her new family. Instead she was here lying like one who was dead.

"I'm sorry," Sally wept over and over again as she begged her aunt to open her eyes.

∼

As if things weren't bad enough for Sally and her aunt, Mrs. Crowe suddenly became hostile towards them. "This isn't a hospital where patients are taken care of," she announced three days after the tragedy. "If your aunt dies in my house, it will create problems for me with not only the police constables, but other tenants as well. I don't want people to think my house is cursed."

"But Mrs. Crowe, where will we go?"

"I think you should take your aunt to the hospital. That's the only place where she can be attended to, and even if she dies there, no one will create any problems. Besides, they will help you to bury her, since you have nothing."

Just like that, they were mercilessly evicted from their dwelling. Mrs. Crowe didn't even allow Sally to pack anything that belonged to them.

"I will bring whatever you own to the hospital. Just be glad that I'm a good Christian and have hired a buggy to take you and your aunt to the hospital. Now hurry, I need to clean this room because I have a new tenant coming to look at the place."

The buggy turned out to be an old cart which smelled horrible, and Sally suspected that it was usually used to carry rubbish and other waste substances, but the man was kind enough to take them up to the hospital, where two burly orderlies carried her aunt into the hospital. It was worse than a nightmare, as the place was packed with sick people.

Sally clutched her aunt's dress as the orderlies carried her and dumped her on the floor of the outpatient department.

"Wait for your turn to see the doctor. What is your mother's name?"

"Anne Cotton," Sally said in a trembling voice. The whole place stank, and she wanted to rush out for fresh air, but she couldn't leave her aunt unattended for fear her aunt would die and no one would look for her. She could hear other patients with rasping coughs, and children cried in pain as their harassed mothers tried to quieten them down. Others had dried blood covering their open wounds and horrible-looking sores that oozed pus.

A few nurses walked around the open space, their handkerchiefs pressed to their noses as if to hold off the terrible stench of human suffering. Sally lay with her head on her aunt's chest and dozed off. Someone kicked her and she quickly sat up, wiping the drool from her lips.

"What is wrong with your mother?"

"Someone hit her. She fell, and she hasn't woken up," she looked up at the nurse, who was staring down at her with sympathy in her eyes. "Please help my mother."

"We'll do everything we can, but are you sure that she's not dead?"

"No, she's not dead."

The nurse took pity on them and called over two orderlies, who carried Anne into one of the consulting rooms where there were four clinical assistants. One of them immediately started examining Anne's throat while another poked and prodded her.

"What is wrong with this patient?" the older of the four assistants asked.

"Her daughter says someone struck her and she hit her head and hasn't woken up."

"For how many days?" Sally noticed that all eyes were on here. "Three days."

"I don't see anything wrong with her, at least not physically, but Sister, can you find a bed for her?" He turned to Sally. "We'll keep your mother overnight, for she might regain consciousness. Then she can tell us what is wrong with her. You wil,l of course, stay with her."

If the outpatient department was filthy, the inpatient ward was ten times worse, but all Sally cared about was the fact that her aunt was given a bed in a corner. The sheets clearly hadn't been changed, and they had blood and other stains, but it was a bed, nonetheless, and once the orderlies and nurse had left, Sally sank down on the bed and closed her eyes in sleep. She was so exhausted, she didn't even care anymore about the horrible smells and groans from other patients.

12

REFUGE AT BEDLAM

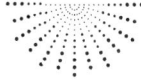

The voice seemed to come from far away, and it was very insistent Anne tried to shut it out, but the person wouldn't stop pleading with her to return. Her mind was mixed up, and she didn't want to open her eyes. Grey shadows swirled about in her mind, and she felt as if she were drowning. She also felt very tired and decided not to respond to the voice calling out to her.

"Aunt Anne, please listen to me. It's me, Sally. Open your eyes and come back to me."

Deciding that even talking took too much of an effort, Anne allowed the other voices in her head to silence this loud one.

Sally was crying as she looked at the doctor who had come to check on her aunt. "What's wrong with my mother?" she asked fearfully. It troubled her greatly that her aunt just lay still, like one who had died. There were about six other student doctors surrounding Aunt Anne's bed, and Sally knew they were there because she was the cleanest patient in the ward. Even with the scarcity of water and the filth all around her, Sally had done her best to ensure that her aunt had a clean place to sleep. She also had to fight for food, even though her aunt barely ate anything.

"Your mother has suffered some trauma, and she is living in another world, as if she isn't here at all."

"How do I bring her back?" the girl asked, taking her aunt's cold hand and chaffing it as if to bring some warmth to it. "Can she hear me?"

The doctor looked at her thoughtfully. He was experienced enough to know that most people who suffered hard blows to the head often developed mental problems. Some of them would get well, but sadly others remained in that state of mind for the rest of their lives. Many of those who got better did so because their loved ones refused to give up on them. Looking at the little girl, he knew that she was the only one who could help his patient.

"Your mother might take time to get well. Do you have other relatives who can help with her care?"

Sally shook her head, "It's just the two of us and I can take care of my mother until she gets better."

"It's obvious that we aren't doing anything for her here, because physically she is not injured. The hospital is full, and all beds are needed for patients in worse condition that your mother. I'm afraid that I'll have to discharge her so you can take her home. She might recover better in familiar surroundings rather than in this place."

"But where will we go?" Sally cried, "Please don't send us away."

"Where were you staying before your mother suffered this terrible accident?"

"With Mrs. Crowe, but she said we can't go back because we don't have any money for the rent." Sally picked up the hem of the frock and blew her nose. "When my mother gets better, we will find work and pay the rent. But she is still ill, and I can't leave her alone to go and work somewhere."

Dr. Christopher Lansing's heart was moved with compassion. "Don't cry, child. Let me see what I can do to help."

"So, we can stay here until my mother gets better?"

"No, but I'm going to find a place for you to live. It won't be a luxurious or even normal place to stay, but your mother will get the help she needs once you get there."

"But I don't have any money to pay."

"You won't have to pay any money at first. Have you heard of Bedlam Women's Mental Hospital?" Sally shook her head. "That is the one place I can think of that will accept your mother in her current condition. After examining her, I have concluded that your mother is suffering from a mental problem."

"Is my mother insane?" Sally asked fearfully. "Has she run mad?"

"No," Dr. Lansing coughed briefly, "Her mind is just tired and needs to rest. I will take you both to Bedlam and see her admitted there, but you have to promise to take care of your mother at all times."

"I promise, "Sally felt a small glimmer of hope. "You said we don't have to pay anything?"

"What I will do is get you into one of the old wards where patients who are not so badly off are cared for. But you will have to find a way of getting some money."

"For what?"

"For your upkeep, both of you. The hospital will be able to care for your mother to a certain point. But you still need to find money for any medication she requires, and also meals. I don't know how the place is run these days, but it's better to be prepared than go there and get surprised."

"I'll do anything," Sally said, quite determined to repay her aunt for all she had done for her. It was her fault that her aunt was ill, and she would work hard to care for her.

"Well, why don't you wait here while I make the necessary arrangements for you?"

"Thank you." Sally felt slightly happier as she watched the doctor and his students move to another patient's bed. They would soon be out of this place, but she refused to complain. At least they would have a place to stay.

It was nearly a week before she saw Dr. Lansing again. It seemed as if he'd forgotten all about them, and she felt relieved, because on the very day she spotted him again, the ward nurse chased Sally and Anne out. At least her aunt had regained consciousness, but she had a blank look in her eyes, and all she did from was grin like an imbecile.

"This woman was supposed to have been discharged a week ago, and I'm surprised you're still here. She is just taking up space in a bed that is needed for someone who is seriously ill."

"But my mother is very ill," Sally pleaded.

"Your mother is just living in her head. Look at her," the nurse pointed out unkindly, "She sits there like a queen ruling over her subjects, saying nothing at all but expecting to be waited on hand and foot."

No matter how much Sally pleaded with the nurse, the woman refused to heed her cries.

"Please find the doctor," Sally pleaded.

"Which doctor?"

"The one who was treating my aunt."

"And what is his name?" The woman's tone was mocking but Sally ignored it. She hadn't caught the doctor's name.

"I don't know it, but if I see him then I can tell you who he is."

Without any mercy at all, Anne was shoved off the bed. Her face was blank, devoid of any expression. Sally wept as she collected their scant belongings in the old tattered bag, held her aunt's hand and led her out of the crowded ward.

They had been here for close to two weeks and had at least had a place to sleep and food to eat. Since the beds were very narrow, Sally had taken to sleeping under the bed, but she never got enough sleep because she was worried about losing her aunt.

Twice Aunt Anne had gotten out of bed and wandered out of the ward. Sally was lucky that, on both occasions, someone had brought her back with a stern warning for Sally to keep an eye on her.

"Don't worry, Aunt Anne, I won't leave you," Sally held her hand, and in the other hand she carried their meagre belongings. Mrs. Crowe had come by and brought them their things and warned Sally not to return to her house.

"I have tenants to care for and I can't have a mad woman roaming the corridors and frightening them and their little ones. Besides, I already found someone to rent your room so there's no place for you in my house again. But I wish you well."

Sally sighed as they stepped out the hospital doors. They had nowhere to go and no money. She knew that her aunt had been keeping some money in the room, but Mrs. Crowe had insisted that their rent was in arrears when Sally asked about the money. Not wanting to get into an argument with the woman, Sally had let it go.

She led her aunt to a stone bench in the park at the front of the hospital. It was really cold, and they didn't have any warm clothing. As she was about to settle down beside her aunt, she spotted Dr. Lansing and shouted, startling him such that he dropped the bag he was carrying.

"Over here," she waved frantically, ignoring the looks of disgust and annoyance of those around. Dr. Lansing also looked angry as he strode towards her.

"What now?"

"You said you would help us," Sally said breathlessly, glad to see him. "I'm sorry for shouting at you."

"I'm sorry that I got caught up with work and clearly forgot. What are you doing out here in the cold?" He stood over Anne, who gave him a blank look. "Has there been any improvement in your mother's condition?"

"No, but the nurse asked us to leave and gave her bed to someone else."

"I told you that would happen." He rubbed his chin.

"You said you would take us to Bedlam." Sally wasn't going to let her last hope walk away. Even an asylum was better than living on the streets. "Please take us there."

"Why don't you let me go inside and attend to a few patients first?"

"No," Sally said daringly, "You will go in there, and something will come up. Then you will forget about us, and we will have to sleep on this bench."

Dr. Lansing chuckled softly. "You're a determined little thing, aren't you?"

"Please," she whispered hoarsely, "I just want my mother to be in a safe place where I can take care of her, so she can get better."

"You've convinced me. Now come along and keep up. I don't have all day, because there are patients waiting for me."

Sally urged Anne to her feet and practically dragged her after the doctor, who stood impatiently beside a buggy outside the hospital gates.

"Hop in and I'll take you there, but once she is admitted, everything else is upon you."

"That is all I need," Sally said.

The doctor didn't look at them all the way to the asylum, but once he had admitted Aunt Anne, Sally clutched his shirt sleeve. "Doctor, thank you very much. You're an angel to us."

Dr. Lansing felt something break within him and his face reddened with guilt. He'd brought this particular patient here so he could get rid of her once and for all. The last thing he'd expected was to be thanked by the beautiful child who looked at him like he had come down from heaven with a miracle for her.

"Here," he dug into his pocket and held out two gold guineas. "These will help you for a few days as you think of how else to take care of your mother." Without another word, he turned and quickly walked out of the asylum, leaving Sally watching him with fear in her eyes. He was the person who had brought them to this place, her only friend for the past few days, and now he had gone, leaving them here.

The walls were all white and stark, and in contrast to how the hospital had been, this place was as quiet as a tomb. At least it didn't smell horrible, only of strong lye.

"You must be the new patient," a woman in her fifties approached them as they sat on the bench on the corridor. "Dr. Lansing said he had brought you here. So, who is the patient?"

"My mother is the one who is ill," Sally pointed at Aunt Anne, who turned and gave the woman a blank smile. "She's been like this for over two weeks. The doctor said there is nothing wrong with her except in her mind."

"Don't worry. You're lucky you came in today when we don't have too many patients to admit, but unfortunately, the rooms we have are all private, and I don't know if you can afford the charges."

"The doctor said he would find us one of the old wards where we wouldn't have to pay as much."

The woman looked slightly irritated. "I don't like it when doctors from outside think they know more about this place than the staff. Wait here."

PART II

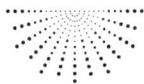

13

THE NEW FRIEND

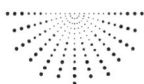

S ally looked around the small room which was to be their home for the unforeseeable future. It hadn't been easy convincing Mrs. Lydia Howe to find them a better place to stay than the old dilapidated ward. In the eyes of the world, the building was just an old barn that was not in use, but that was where the poorest of the poor were practically dumped and forgotten. Even the pigs at the Manor had a better sty than this place. The moment Sally had seen the place, she'd recoiled with horror and begged Mrs. Howe to consider finding them a different place to stay. After much thought, and after making Sally aware of how much of a favour she was doing for them, she brought them to this room. It was a small room at the end of one of the old but slightly better wards than the one Sally thought of as a cowshed.

"This used to be one of the rooms used by the nurses," Mrs. Howe told her. "But since better quarters were provided for the nurses, this room has been empty."

Tears filled Sally's eyes when she looked at the deplorable state of the room. There were two beds in the room, and she could see that the second one was occupied. She had left her aunt at the reception because Mrs. Howe had asked her to.

"Did you say the room is supposed to be empty?" Mrs. Howe nodded. "This bed seems to have someone sleeping in it." Sally didn't want to imagine her aunt being in the same room with someone else, especially if it was a man. From the way she'd seen things around the asylum, the poor patients were neglected. If the person was a man, he might attack her aunt.

Mrs. Howe frowned and walked to the bed. "I know that sometimes the cleaners put the dirty laundry in here, especially when there's no water, but I didn't think there could be a person in here. I thought it was just the usual pile of beddings."

"No, it's a person."

Mrs. Howe looked down at the person and sighed in exasperation. "It's you again," she practically dragged the person, a dirty-looking woman, out of the bed and threw her to the floor. "How many times have I told you not to come into this room? Who let you in when there was a lock on the door?"

The woman grinned at her, looking like a total imbecile, and crawled toward the door. She sat on the threshold and started singing a nonsensical song. Sally noticed that she had a piece of wood wrapped in a dirty cloth and was rocking it like one would a baby.

"Don't worry, I'll get rid of her in a moment," Mrs. Howe said. "Do you think your mother will be all right in this room? But just so you know, this is a sort of special room so..-" her voice faded, and Sally got the idea that she expected payment of some sort.

"Can I stay here and look after my mother please?"

"Family can only visit, and I'm being generous by allowing you to even come this far. Usually we admit patients at the reception, and then the orderlies and nurses bring them to the wards without their families. The only time they get to see their families is once a week. You're lucky I took pity on you. But your mother should be all right here alone. I promise to look after her."

Sally knew that if she left Aunt Anne, the poor woman wouldn't make it. She would definitely be neglected, just like the other poor patients she'd seen.

"I have some money," Sally whispered, "Please, can you help me find a position here? I can clean and do laundry, as well as cook."

She saw the woman's eyes light up with greed.

"How much?"

"I have two gold guineas.," That was the money Dr. Lansing had pressed into her hand before his hasty exit from the asylum. "But I will work hard and continue giving you more money. Please don't send me away, because I don't have a home. We lost our home when my mother got sick, and I've been taking care of her at the hospital until the doctor brought us here."

The woman actually licked her lips. "Let me see what I can do. Now give me the money." She held out her hand.

Sally shook her head. "Keep your end of the bargain, and I'll do the same." She knew that she was taking a huge risk. "Allow me to work here, and I will do anything you want."

"Young girl, you realize that I could just as well take everything away from you." Even though Sally saw the anger in Mrs. Howe's eyes, she also saw something else like respect.

"But you're an honourable woman and won't do it. And I know that I will help you in many other ways. You see, when I was at the hospital taking care of my mother, I used to wash the clothes for some of the other patients, and they paid me so I could buy food and pay for my mother's medicine. Whatever work you need done and can't do yourself, I'll do it, and if there is any money to be made, I will share a portion of it with you. Please allow me to take care of my mother."

Lydia frowned. This chit of a girl was too shrewd for her own good. But Lydia was also crafty enough to realise that she could have someone to run those errands she eschewed. Being a public asylum with a private wing, Lydia had often dealt with patients whose families were willing to pay any amount of money for their care. Sadly, those same family members didn't want to be the ones to provide the care, and as the institution was often overflowing with patients, the nurses, their assistants and orderlies were swamped. In any case, even though every staff member worked very hard, times were difficult, and it was a case of everyone looking out for themselves. If she had a little lapdog who was eager to please, then she could make a lot of money from the patients. So, she smiled at Sally, who chose to ignore the avarice in the woman's eyes.

"Very well then, I will allow you to stay here. But just make sure that you obey all my instructions and make sure that you only listen to me." Though the woman's words sounded odd and her voice quite intimidating, Sally didn't want to lose this chance. "Come with me to get your mother. I hope she hasn't wandered off, but not to worry, someone will find her and bring her back if she has." Mrs. Howe stepped out of the small room, and then she frowned as she looked at the woman who was still muttering to herself. "I need to get rid of this one."

There was something about the other woman that touched Sally. She was holding her piece of wood close to her heart as she rocked back and forth. "Oliver," she crooned, and Sally gave a start.

"Oliver?"

Mrs. Howe waved a dismissive hand, "Ignore this one, who has been here forever. I came to this institution ten years ago and found her here. No one knows who she is or where she came from."

"Doesn't she have any family?" Sally couldn't imagine anyone abandoning their family member.

"If she had any family, they have since stopped coming to visit her. She usually doesn't bother anyone, so we let her stay, but she is really filthy. Once in a while we clean her up, but she only gets herself filthy once again. We have too much to do around here, and since she isn't violent or anything, we just leave her alone. But if you're to take over this room, then I will have to make her realise that she can't come here anymore."

"No," Sally shook her head, looking at the woman with compassion. "If you say she's not a bother, then let her stay. This room can contain us all."

Mrs. Howe gave Sally an odd look, "You are really a strange child. Are you sure that you want to be taking on an extra burden when you already have your mother to care for?"

"She might be good company for my mother."

"You are a funny one," Mrs. Howe said. "But if you allow her to stay in this room with you, then you have to be ready to take over caring for her. This means making sure that she is cleaned regularly and gets all her meals. As it is, since no one really bothers about her, the cooks just usually give her whatever is left over after everyone else has been served."

Sally thought Mrs. Howe was an odd woman indeed. She was greedy for gain, yes, but beneath all that avarice there was some measure of kindness. The woman wasn't a hopeless case.

"I promise that I will do it," Sally said, smiling at the grinning woman, who gave her a smile showing yellow teeth. She stank, but Sally had dealt with worse at the hospital. Taking care of one more woman who was only filthy wasn't really a problem. At the hospital, she'd dealt with patients who had festering wounds and terrible injuries, and she'd survived.

∾

It was Friday evening, three days before Christmas, and the whole hospital was abuzz with activities ranging from decorating the dining hall where the mild patients took their meals, to personalised ones in the rooms of those who could afford them.

Sally and Aunt Anne had been in Bedlam for about three years now, and things had settled down into some sort of routine. While the place was far from the kind of life she would have wanted to live, it was still home. Mrs. Lydia Howe had sort of become her friend Sally carried out all manner of errands for the woman, and the payment she got was good food at least twice a week for her and her charges. Mrs. Howe would also give her three shillings every Friday as her weekly wages, which Sally kept tied up in a small scarf and hidden under Aunt Anne's pillow for safekeeping. No one entered their small room or bothered them, and Sally knew that it was because, in her own strange way, Mrs. Howe was looking out for them.

Sally had just returned from cleaning a wealthy patient's room and been given the previous day's food, which consisted of mashed potatoes, some beef cubes, and thick gravy and she was feeling tired. The food was cold, and bacon fat had congealed around it. and because it was the patient's food, was rather bland. But it was still edible and better than what was being served in the common dining hall. Aunt Anne had turned her back the moment Sally entered the room and tried to get her to eat. On a good day, she would feed herself, even though she made a little bit of a mess, but there were times when she became difficult and Sally had to feed her. Today was one of those days.

"Aunt Anne, please, you have to eat something. I don't want you to get ill and die. I promise that when you're better, we'll get out of here." Anne didn't respond. "Christmas Day is coming up in three days, and I promise that I will take you for a walk. Do you remember how you took me to the London Bridge a few years ago on Christmas Day? We saw horses and people dressed in fancy clothes, and you promised that you would one day buy me a beautiful frock. Aunt Anne, I want you to get better so you can buy me that frock."

Anne turned around and slowly sat up, her eyes fixed on Sally's. The young girl had no idea if her aunt understood her, because her eyes were blank, but Mrs. Howe had told her to never stop talking about normal things to her aunt.

"Thank you for sitting up. Now please open your mouth, and I will help you eat your dinner."

Anne opened her lips and accepted the mushy food, grimacing at the bland taste, but Sally was thankful that she didn't spit it out. When she was done feeding her aunt, she wiped her mouth and helped her to lie back down. "Please let me check on Mrs. Jane," she whispered, referring to her second charge. Since she didn't know the woman's real name, the young girl had taken to calling her Mrs. Jane. Sally stood there and watched her aunt as she closed her eyes. A few minutes later, she was asleep and deep sadness tore at the young girl's heart. Her aunt seemed so fragile, a far cry from the robust and beautiful woman that she had been before.

Quickly dashing her tears away, she hurried to the other side of the room and gently shook the other woman awake.

"Mrs. Jane, I brought you some food."

The woman opened her eyes and then stared at Sally. "My son," she looked around wildly, "Where is Oliver?" She sat up quickly and looked around, her eyes darting to and fro. "Oliver, where are you?"

"Here," Sally was careful never to touch the piece of wood that the woman insisted was her son. Sally pointed at the piece of wood on Jane's pillow. "He's sleeping, so you need to eat something and be strong, so you can take care of him."

Mrs. Jane nodded and allowed Sally to feed her.

When both women were asleep, the young girl quickly cleaned the small room. She couldn't believe how lucky they had been to get this room. Even though Lydia collected half her wages, the woman looked out for the three of them.

Sally couldn't believe that she was turning fifteen in two months' time. Three years in this place and her aunt didn't seem to be getting better. She wondered if this was how she'd spend the rest of her life.

≈

Oliver knew that with everyone safely in bed, this was the best time for him to visit the dungeons. He had no idea why the man who was in chains down there continued to draw him. There was something about that prisoner that got to him every time. Even with everything that had happened to him in the past few years, he found that he couldn't stay away from the dark underground, and the man he had come to think of as Mr. Cage because of his current habitation.

Many years had gone by, but the man still languished in the dungeon. Oliver had even asked if he could find someone to help free him, but the man had been emphatic about never letting anyone know about him. This made Oliver wonder if the man wasn't punishing himself for something and believed that languishing in the dungeon was his penance. In any case, Oliver had honoured his wishes and kept his secret all these years. Oliver knew that he didn't have to keep coming back to visit him, but there was another reason that he did. Every time he came down here, it reminded him of Sally. This stranger in the dungeon was his one connection with Sally, and that was something he didn't want to ever lose.

"Why do you keep coming back here even when I have asked you plenty of times not to continue doing so?" Mr. Cage asked when Oliver had passed him the package of food. He'd brought him some fresh bread and roasted boar that he'd caught a few days ago. "You have a life out there, and I fear that one day the bad people who put me here will catch you. When they do, you can be sure that they'll not hesitate to hurt you since you know of my existence."

"Sir, won't you at least tell me your name, your real one at least?"

"Why would you want to know it after all this time?"

"Just so I can know what to call you," Oliver replied. "I need to call you something"

The man smiled, "Why would you want to call me anything? I hope you're not talking to anyone about me?"

"No,sir , but I just wondered."

"Don't you worry a thing about that; just continue calling me whatever you have been until now."

"But-"

"Young man, do you realise that I don't even know your name, nor do I want to? Let us not go into too many details about names, because they don't matter. But all I can say is that I'm very grateful for your help all these years. Still, I have to ask you why you have kept coming. The last thing I want is for you to get into trouble."

Oliver shrugged, "I'm always very careful and Tubby here always warns me if someone is coming," he pointed at the cat who was scratching herself in the corner. Her movements seemed slower these days, and Oliver knew that his cat was growing old.

"Still, I don't understand why you care so much about a prisoner like me. I'm nothing to you, and I believe you could be doing better things than skulking here in the underground like a hermit. If you stopped coming to see me, I wouldn't hold it against you."

To Oliver, the man's words made sense, but he was like family to him. As much as he wanted to tell him about feeling closer to Sally by being here, he kept silent. And the man's next question surprised him. It was as though he'd read Oliver's mind.

"What happened to that little girl who used to accompany you years ago when you would come to the dungeons? What was her name again?"

Oliver frowned, "You've never asked about her before."

Mr. Cage looked aside then back at Oliver. "From the moment your little friend stopped accompanying you, I noticed a difference in your demeanour. I didn't want to hurt your feelings because I could see that even as children the two of you were very close. When she stopped coming, I thought maybe she'd fallen ill and died. You've been very sad for years."

Oliver acknowledged this to be true. "Sally and her aunt left many years ago, and I don't know what happened to her because she's never returned."

"Have you ever thought about going out there to look for her?"

Oliver looked at the man incredulously, "The only thing I know about her is her name, and even that only the first one which is Salome or Sally. So where would I even start searching for her?"

"I don't know," Mr. Cage shrugged. "If you have enough faith, anything is possible."

"Speaking of faith, don't you have any left in you?"

"I'm alive, aren't I? Being in this palace of mine," his voice was full of mockery, "I have been down here in darkness for years, and if I can count, it has been about eighteen years now."

"How can you tell?"

"Just a feeling. How old are you son?"

"Seventeen going on eighteen. Why?"

"Just wondering, and do you still live in the house upstairs?"

Oliver shook his head, "I left some years ago." He didn't want to go into the whole story about how he'd run away years ago and ended up living in the forest like a Gypsy.

"So, where do you live now?"

"In the forest."

"How then do you get down here these days?"

"There are many routes, and after all this is a dungeon with many tunnels leading in many different directions." Oliver walked around the cell. "I've been taking time to follow the tunnels as far as they go, and there are many of them. It's a labyrinth down here. Did you know that one of them goes right down to the sea? I haven't gone that deep out, but I remember hearing waves from a distance, so I assumed that it was the sea. There seems to have been a cave-in because that tunnel is blocked and didn't break out to the coast."

The man looked startled. "You've got to be very careful because this dungeon and the tunnels must have been used by smugglers in the past. This manor is really old, and maybe the owners' ancestors were smugglers. The smugglers might still be using these dungeons as their hideout, or worse, criminals who are running away from the law. Please don't continue coming down here, because you could one day run into them and they would hurt you really badly."

Oliver gave Mr. Cage an odd look. "You seem to know a lot about this house. Did you ever live in it?" Maybe the man had been a servant who did something terrible to his parents and was then locked up down here. Or he might be one of the smugglers that he spoke of. Maybe he'd crossed his partners in crime, and this was the punishment they felt was fit for him. "Or are you one of the smugglers?"

"No," Mr. Cage laughed and scratched his scruffy beard. "I'm just assuming that because many old mansions like this one had tunnels beneath them and passages in the walls leading from all the rooms of the house. For centuries, battles have been fought on the soil of England, and people had different allegiances when it came to politics and religion. They needed to have places to hide themselves, their families, and other valuables until the perils were past. If trouble struck, they could easily slip into the passageways in the walls through their bedrooms and other rooms in the house, find their way to these tunnels, and hide out here or escape to safety."

Oliver had the feeling that the man wasn't quite telling him the truth, but before he could ask any further questions, Tubby came rushing towards the cell and hissing.

"I have to go," he grabbed the wrappings in which he'd carried Mr. Cage's food and disappeared into the dark tunnel. He was just in time, for he heard voices coming down the opposite tunnel.

14
PRECIOUS MEMORIES

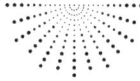

C hristmas came and went, and the residents of Bedlam carried on with their lives. Spring was nigh, and the weather was getting warmer, which Sally was thankful for. Some patients got better and were discharged, and Sally gazed longingly at them as their families received them back into the fold. Some other patients died and were carried away on the old hearse that came to the institution three times a week to collect the dead. During such times, Sally cried softly as she watched the lifeless bodies being lifted from the hospital's gurney and placed carefully at the back of the cart. Sometimes there was just one body, but usually it was three or four. It broke her heart when she thought about those poor creatures who had no families and would have to be buried by the city council workers in unmarked graves.

She purposed in her heart that her aunt wouldn't be one of those who was carried out at the back of a cart. Aunt Anne would get better, she just had to. Usually after watching the dead being carried away, Sally would mope for hours, and during such times she wandered outside, not wanting to meet with anyone and staying away from their small room. Her aunt and Mrs. Jane were very sensitive to her moods, and if she went to the room with a downcast face, the two women would start crying, and it would take a while before they calmed down. They were like twins, feeding off each other's emotions, and Sally was careful to only present a happy face to them.

The small garden at the back of the large kitchen where the clothes lines were fixed was beautiful, though choked with weeds. Sally liked coming out here and spending some time while hanging out the laundry. One spring morning, she couldn't take the ugliness of the garden anymore, so she finished hanging the sheets, put the wooden pail aside, and knelt at the edge of the garden. She began pulling the weeds out, wishing she had a gardening trowel or hand fork to make her work easier. Someone should look after this pretty garden, which if well-tended, could bring so much joy and peace to the patients. Aunt Anne and Mrs. Jane were taking their mid-morning naps, and she had some free time before going to help out in the kitchen.

Because she was very young, Mrs. Howe was careful not to give her difficult tasks that might overwhelm her. Sally knew that the woman was giving her a special measure of grace, and even though she had to give her nearly half of her wages, she didn't mind. Sally had accidentally found out from one of the other nurses that she was actually liable to be paid by the institution, but Mrs. Howe pocketed whatever was due her and continued giving her three shillings every Friday. Knowing that complaining could only lead to trouble made Sally remain silent. In any case, she had no one to report it to, since the only administrator she knew of was Mrs. Howe.? It was better to remain silent and live on whatever they had than lose it all. *"Half a loaf is better than none,"* Mrs. Howe had once told her.

"What are you doing?" Miss Lydia shouted from a window on the first floor of a building across from where Sally was working. "I'm coming down right now," and she disappeared from sight, but Sally knew she would soon be with her. She sat back on her haunches and wondered if she was in any kind of trouble as she waited for the woman to come down to her She turned when the footsteps came closer.

"I'm just pulling out a few weeds to make the place beautiful," Sally said, waving a hand at the garden. "There are some very pretty flowers that can bloom if well-tended, and the patients could do with some beauty in their lives. I usually bring my mother and Mrs. Jane out here to get some sunshine, and it would be nice for them to see the pretty flowers and enjoy some beauty in their otherwise bleak lives."

"No one is going to pay you for doing that kind of work. And I would have thought that you have enough to do without burdening yourself with what you haven't been asked to do."

"I'm not looking to be paid for doing this. I just finished hanging out the laundry and decided to pull up a few weeds. If I pull up a few each day, the garden will soon look pretty again," Sally's voice was husky. She'd had a really trying day with her aunt and Mrs. Jane, and she was glad that they were asleep.

When her aunt had been admitted to the asylum three years ago, Sally had thought that they would be here for just a few days, at most a month or two. But three years had gone by now, and Aunt Anne didn't seem to be getting any better. While she wasn't getting any worse, it was still very disheartening to see the blank look in her eyes, day after day. And what's worse, the last doctor who had seen her had been by over eight months ago.

"There's nothing wrong with your mother," he said. "I believe she is just one of those lazy patients who doesn't want to get better." The man's tone was quite scathing and bruised Sally's heart. "It beats me why anyone would want to be stuck in this place, but I guess we all have our preferences." Sally had wished that she could scream at him. No one else had come to see her aunt.

"You look sad," Mrs. Howe said, moving to lean against a rickety post. "What's going on with you? Has anyone harmed you?"

The one thing Sally was most glad for about her strange and unusual friendship with Mrs. Howe was the fact that the woman made it clear to all the male staff at the institution that none of them was to touch Sally or molest her in any way. That kept her safe, even though she was also very careful about her personal security. It was one thing for the administrator to warn the men from attacking her, but she wasn't always around, and Sally took no chances.

Sally put her knees back on the ground and looked up at the older woman. "Will my mother ever get better?" She had told everyone that Aunt Anne was her mother. No one disputed the fact because they looked so much alike. "Will we ever walk out of here with her being normal, or is this it for her? Will my mother die in here without ever getting better?"

Lydia sighed, folding her hands across her chest. "Child, I always tell those who care for patients that they should take it one day at a time and that's how they should live. Don't go borrowing trouble, and as the good Book says, sufficient for today are its own problems, and you don't need to add those of tomorrow to it."

"But she is not receiving any treatment, and she hasn't been for the last eight months. The last doctor said she's just one of those lazy patients who don't want to get better," Sally's tone was full of indignation.

"Child, don't get all bristled up like that. Be glad that your mother is healthy and safe, thanks to you. Your mother is not at all lazy, and I'm sorry that doctor said that to you."

"Then why isn't she getting better? Is it something I'm not doing right?"

"Not at al., I understand your anxieties. It's not that you're not taking good care of your mother. You need to be patient with yourself. Don't overwork yourself just so your mother can get better. Taking care of her and making her feel loved is all she needs right now."

"But when will she get better?" Sally felt the tears behind her eyes.

Mrs. Lydia shook her head slowly., "I don't know, but please don't agitate yourself thinking about matters that only the Lord can deal with. At least your mother doesn't have any other underlying illnesses. Be thankful for small mercies, and count your blessings."

"Yes, Mrs. Howe."

~

Miles away, Oliver was trying very hard to count his blessings, but he was failing miserably. Living as a vagabond wasn't much of a life. Even Gypsies lived in communities and had families. He had no one, hadn't had anyone to call his family for years now, except Tubby. He was still surprised that his mother believed that he would hurt his own father. While he knew that he should be thankful for being alive after all the troubles he'd endured over the years, he still felt like he'd been cheated by life, especially because his own parents and siblings had turned against him.

Even now, years later, the accusations still hurt. For as long as he lived, he would never forget his mother referring to him as the devil's spawn. No mother should call her own child that! His brother and sister enjoyed the luxury of their parents' house while he lived in the woods like a Gypsy. Mercifully, no one had ever come looking for him again, or had found out that he was hiding out in the thick forest.

He met hunters and woodcutters in the forest, but as long as he didn't interfere with their traps or get in their way, they also didn't bother him.

He sat on the small porch, stroking Tubby's back slowly. His cat was dying, and he was really sad. She had been his companion for about nine years, and he'd never seen her with any kittens even though he'd suspected her to be pregnant many times before. It was as if Tubby didn't want anything else to take Oliver's attention away from her, not even her own kittens.

"What will I do without you, Tubby?" he asked, forcing himself not to cry. He was eighteen, a man now, and he didn't think it was manly for him to be shedding tears, certainly not over a cat. But apart from Mr. Cage, Tubby was the only other family he knew, and she'd kept him company in this small woodcutter's hut for years.

Tubby struggled to get to her feet and then collapsed once again with her head on his lap. Her breathing was laboured, and Oliver knew she didn't have long to live.

"If only Sally were here," he murmured to Tubby. "She would help me with this pain of knowing that you're going to be gone soon." He wiped his eyes. "You've been my friend for so long. How will I cope without you? And Mr. Cage will miss you too, because you've kept rats and other crawling creatures out of his cell for years."

Tubby once again raised her head and struggled to her feet, her whole body trembling. "Where are you going?" Oliver asked, watching as she went down the steps then stopped and turned to look at him as if urging him to follow her. "What is it?" Oliver followed her as she walked on shaky fours until they got behind the hut. She moved under the small bush and meowed. Oliver knelt down and peered into the bushes, not hesitating at all because he was sure there were no reptiles or harmful creatures lurking there. Tubby kept their surrounding free of harmful creatures.

"Oh, Tubby," Oliver said half crying and half laughing. "What did you do?" Oliver saw two fat kittens sleeping in the nest clearly made by Tubby to protect her young. "I finally get to meet your little ones." Oliver didn't want to leave the kittens in the bushes. "May I pick them up and take them to the house?" And as he said this, he picked them up one by one and Tubby didn't object.

Once he got to the cabin, he poured out the last of the milk on a tin plate, then pushed it toward the kittens. He then picked Tubby up and sat with her on his lap, and the two of them watched the kittens as they lapped the milk.

"Your children are very beautiful, Tubby," he gently stroked her head and smiled. If anyone heard him talking to a cat, they would most definitely think that he was insane. "Thank you for sharing them with me." He watched the kittens for a while, then realised that Tubby had gone very still. Her breathing was no longer laboured, and he frowned slightly. She wasn't breathing at all.

"Tubby?" He gently raised her and looked into her face. Her eyes were shut, and she was still, and he realised that she was gone forever. Gently lowering her back on his lap, he wiped his tears. "Thank you for giving me two beautiful babies to replace you. Rest well, dear friend." He looked at the kittens, which didn't seem to know what was going on or that their mother was gone forever. "Sally would have really loved you two," Oliver said, letting the tears flow.

$$\approx$$

"Oh, Oliver," Sally lay on the floor, listening to her two charges. "I wish you were here to help me through this." She let the tears fall on the sides of her face. She was so lonely, and she wished that her good friend was here with her. She thought about what he might be doing now, and if he ever thought about her. Many years had passed, and she wondered if he had forgotten about her. She would never stop missing him and Tubby too.

She felt the cold as she lay on the thin mattress on the floor, but there was no extra blanket. Whatever linens she'd been given went to her charges. They needed all the warmth they could get in this small cold room. Many times, Sally wished she could build a fire to keep the room warm, but the smoke would kill them all since the window was tiny and locked most of the time to keep the cold out.

Yet she refused to complain. "Count my blessings," she muttered, recalling what Mrs. Lydia had told her a few weeks ago. Having this small room to themselves was bliss. It was their haven, and they didn't have to share it with anyone else or mix with the other patients. Although it was small and drafty, it was theirs alone.

She turned on her side, wishing she could get more comfortable, but the old mattress Lydia had found from somewhere, of course at a small price, was threadbare, and she could feel the cold seeping through. Knowing that she wouldn't get sleep anytime soon, she sat up and leaned against the door. Raising her legs, she placed her chin on her knees and wrapped her arms around them.

She was hungry, and her stomach growled to attest to that, but there was nothing to eat until tomorrow. She could, of course, sneak down to the kitchen and steal something. There was always some leftover food, and she knew this because she washed the pots in the morning and found it. But the last time she'd gone down to the kitchen at night, she had nearly gotten into a lot of trouble. She had managed to escape being assaulted by the night guards, and she'd never ventured out of the room at night and alone again.

"This is a really hard life," she let her tears flow. She worried that she would eventually go out of her mind. "I have to be strong for Aunt Anne and Mrs. Jane," she sniffed softly. Her aunt had been there for her ever since her own parents died years ago, and now it was her turn to take care of her. And she would do it without a murmur, even if it took the rest of her life. She owed Aunt Anne that much.

∾

At twenty-one, Maeve Winchester was no roaring beauty, but she had a certain appeal that she used to her full advantage. There was a fire burning within , especially when she espied her brother's best friend Clifton Fanwood. It didn't matter that Cliff, as he preferred to be called, was about thirty years old, much older than her or Kent. He was handsome and very charming, and the first time Kent brought him home, Maeve had the feeling that her brother feared his friend.

Rather than put her off, since she was very close with her brother, she found that she quite liked a man who looked strong and who had a mind of his own. Her mother also seemed to like him, and she couldn't resist batting her eyelids at him whenever he happened to glance in her direction. But he was also the soul of discretion and never went out of his way to be found alone in a room with her.

It frustrated her that the man seemed to go out of his way to avoid her, and yet she was quite enamoured of him. While growing up, she'd done her fair share of flirting with the stable boys and Kent's other friends, but it was only mild attraction on her part, even though the young men seemed to take her seriously. It seemed like each month she received no less than four or five proposals of marriage from lusty young men who professed their undying love for her. She would read each beautifully penned note and then shred it, tossing the bits into the fire in her bedchamber. Then she would lie on her bed and laugh at their feeble attempts to get her to respond to their childish displays of love and adoration for her.

Then there were those who sent her flowers and other trinkets as gifts, which she, of course, kept, for every young woman likes receiving gifts. But her heart was cold and well-preserved in her breast. It was like she was holding out for something bigger, something better. That was until she saw Cliff, and then she was lost.

It didn't help matters that Cliff was a very skilled sailor, and he wasn't humble about his pursuits. He spoke of his endeavours, and she listened with bated breath, imagining the wind blowing through his hair and him looking like a handsome gentleman pirate. Then she would dream about him for days on end, sighing with longing and staring out of her window to await his return whenever he was away with Kent.

"My brothers and I have crossed the English Channel countless times," he boasted to them one time, "And each time I have steered our boat safely across."

Maeve's eyes goggled as she imagined the wind passing through Cliff's thick dark hair. She was fascinated by everything about Cliff and thought he was one of those very finely sculptured men, even a god perhaps. Whenever he smiled in her direction, she felt as if her insides were melting, and she knew that she would die if he didn't marry her, but he didn't seem romantically attracted to her, or perhaps he was only pretending. She had to find out from Kent if she stood a chance with the man at all.

❧

"Your sister is a very beautiful young lady," Cliff told Kent not many days later as they were sailing leisurely across the channel. It was one of those beautiful summer days in which the sun was not too hot and the breeze was just gentle enough to tickle the skin. Bristol was a tourist destination, and many people came from London for the good weather and to enjoy the beach. Because he didn't want to mix with the other tourists, Cliff had asked Kent to accompany him for a sail.

"Isn't she a little bit too young for you?" Kent asked, his eyes darting all around as they stood at the railing. They could still see the beach, and Kent's chest puffed out when he imagined all the beautiful women staring at him as he sailed on this luxurious yacht. "And besides, my mother was talking about Maeve soon being betrothed to someone else, so my parents would never consent to a union between the two of you." This was said with much arrogance, which was quickly disguised because Kent needed to be in the good graces of the older man.

Cliff was clearly very wealthy, and Kent needed money urgently. He'd made the mistake of getting involved with an older woman, who introduced him to the vice of gambling, and he was now in very deep. Already the people he owed money to were threatening him with dire consequences, but he had the protection of Cliff, whom he'd met in one of the gambling dens. Cliff never gambled, but he told Kent that he liked to watch people losing money.

Cliff trained his grey eyes on the man he despised with his whole heart, but Kent was a vital part of the plans he had for his life, and he didn't let his feelings of contempt show. Even though he had many other vices, gambling and drinking weren't included, and he could never stand a man who couldn't hold his liquor or one who carelessly lost his money at gaming tables. Still, it was good business for him because he was a moneylender without any conscience whatsoever.

He had it on good authority that Kent Winchester was heir to a vast estate which was asset rich but cash poor. According to the same source, Kent's father had been in some sort of accident which had rendered him impotent and unable to discharge his duties on the estate. Kent, as the oldest son, had taken over the estate and run it to the ground. Seeing that he'd made a mess of things, he started secretly selling off some of the valuable items, but his mother had soon caught wind of his doings and threatened to disinherit him unless he restored the estate's fortunes. Kent started gambling, small amounts at first, and like any new person in the game, he got cockier as he won, placing larger bets each time. Then the crash came, and the losses began. That's when he'd come to Cliff's attention.

Clifton had been born on the wrong side of the tracks, and he had deep hatred for the wealthy because his own father, according to his maternal grandmother, had been very rich but had disowned him and his mother. The man, who his grandmother had refused to reveal to him, had seduced his sixteen-year-old mother, who was working as a maid in his household. When she conceived, he and his wife then chased her away. She died giving birth to him, her heart and body both broken. Life in his grandmother's household was tough for young Cliff ,as his uncles called him an outsider. The beatings and starving, instead of killing him in body and spirit, made him all the more determined to succeed. At the age of ten, he ran away from home and ended up in the underworld of London, attaching himself to a certain Madam who turned him into her personal slave, but he knew what he was after, and at the age of twenty-one, he secretly murdered his mistress and inherited all her wealth, which was vast. After that, he sought all the wealthy men he could find, and using various methods of compromise, blackmailed them into becoming his financial slaves.

In the underworld, and even with many influential men of London, Clifton's name struck terror into men's hearts, turning them feeble and malleable to his well-crafted ploys. He knew their secrets,—even those whispered in the bedchambers,—and used them to manipulate them into doing whatever he required. Many paid for his silence, and the few who didn't soon found themselves exposed and humiliated in public. Two high-ranking officials in Queen Victoria's court found themselves in dire straits when blackmailed by Clifton, and they took the only way out they could, by ending their own lives.

Clifton's interest in Kent was because of his father's large estate in Bristol. What the industrious Cliff wanted was to turn the estate into a country club because it was near the beach, though the coastline was rugged and not fit for any ships or boats to land. His deepest desire for acquiring the vast Winchester Estate was because he knew that it had a dungeon and tunnels leading right to the sea, a smuggler's haven. By possessing and owning the estate, he could control a lot of the smuggling and add to his wealth. That was the reason he befriended the gullible and unsuspecting Kent.

"I do believe that a young woman should be allowed to choose her spouse based on her feelings for him and not because of his position in life," Cliff said. "You're of age now, and since your father is indisposed, I believe you're the man of the house," Cliff shifted his stance and drew closer to Kent. "I'm enamoured of your sister, and my heart yearns for her. It would be worth your while if you would stand in on my behalf and beg your parents to allow me to be her beloved husband. This could be a gentleman's arrangement between you and me."

Kent's greedy eyes lit up and he gave Cliff a sly look. "What kind of arrangement do you have in mind?"

15

IN SEARCH OF THE TRUTH

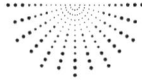

S ally found herself in a kind of agony. She missed Oliver and wondered where he was. He would be eighteen now and probably very handsome. She wondered if he thought of her, or if she had been forgotten. Nine years was a long time to be away from someone.

They had been children when they parted on that terrible morning that Mr. Winchester had attacked her aunt.

"Oh, Oliver," she muttered, "where are you, my love?" Then she stopped, as she was only fifteen and had no business thinking about matters of the heart. Her aunt and Mrs. Jane needed her to be sane, not a dreamer. As she paused in her wanderings, the young woman realised that she was in the newest ward of the hospital. She knew that she wasn't supposed to be in this particular ward and had chosen a time when the doctors and nurses were done with their rounds. She heard voices coming her way and unsuccessfully tried to find a place to hide because she recognized one of those as Mrs. Howe's.

"And if you come this way, I will show you our private wing." Mrs. Howe was talking to a tall, well-dressed gentleman, and Sally deduced that he was the guardian of a prospective patient. She pressed herself against the wall, praying that the woman wouldn't pay any attention to her. This ward was a forbidden area to her because only the wealthy were admitted here. Mrs. Howe had warned her never to set foot in this place, but Sally just couldn't keep away. For one, the corridors were wide and well lit, as were the rooms. Each patient had a cozy room, and they were allowed to have their servants here taking care of them.

Sally liked coming up here because the servants would often request her to run errands for them. Though they never paid her in cash, they did so in kind, and she was able to get tidbits to make their own small room look better and more like home. Sometimes she also got stale buns and bread and rotting fruit, but she wasn't one to complain. After all, beggars couldn't be choosers, and the leftovers she got from their fancy patients were far better than what was served in the kitchen.

As Mrs. Howe and her visitor passed by, Sally felt uncomfortable at the way the man looked at her. Once they had gone, she dashed back downstairs and out of the building and headed toward familiar ground.

Though it was spring, it was still very cold, and Sally needed warm clothing and bedding for her charges. She worried about their health, and that was the reason she'd strayed to the private ward. Someone had put out a large wooden crate on the first floor of the three-storied building. Old clothes and bedding from the rooms of the wealthy were often dumped into this crate, and whoever got there first would find items that were in good condition. Sally always strove to be the first because once or twice she had found nearly new clothes, which she had then sold to have money to take care of her aunt and Mrs. Jane, but she hadn't gotten to the box today and would have to return later.

~

The corridor was empty, and Sally breathed a sigh of relief. She had waited for two hours, during which she fed her charges and watched them take their afternoon nap before making a return trip. Once she ascertained that the corridor was empty, she quickly made her way to the large box. There was no time to sort through each item there, and she grabbed as many as she could.

Just as she was passing by one of the private rooms on her way back to her own part of the institution, the tall gentleman she'd seen earlier being shown around by Mrs. Howe emerged, and she bumped into him. He reached out his hands to her shoulders and steadied her.

"Why are you in such a hurry," his voice was deep and pleasant. "My name is Edgar Gillen. I saw you earlier, but you fled before I could speak with you."

"Why?" she clutched the garments closer to her chest and stepped back. The man's nearness unnerved her. He smelled of tobacco and sandalwood, which wasn't unpleasant. But Sally had been very careful not to get close to any men, not even those who worked at their institution. She could never forget how Mr. Winchester had attacked her aunt and torn her dress, intending her terrible harm and humiliation.

Also, once they moved to London, Aunt Anne had told her over and over again to be careful around men.

"They can hurt you very badly and destroy your life," Aunt Anne had said.

So even as she found the much-older Edgar to be pleasant, she was still very wary of him.

"You don't have to be afraid, because I mean you no harm. I brought in my aunt who is sick. Aunt Matilda is my mother's elder sister and she brought me up when my parents died. But for the past four months, she hasn't been quite herself."

"I'm sorry to hear that," Sally mumbled.

"Do you work here?"

"Yes and no," Sally said cryptically, casting glances around just in case Mrs. Howe was close by. She felt her face flushing at the way his intense gaze seemed to be pinned on her. "Please, may I leave now? I'm not supposed to be here, and if caught, I will be in a lot of trouble." She moved out of his light embrace but he captured her hand.

"I'll only let you go when you tell me your name."

"It's Salome."

"Just one name?"

"Salome Cotton. Please, I have to go," and she dashed away, unaware that Edgar was staring after her, a thoughtful look in his eyes.

∼

Sally was rinsing a large pile of washing in the laundry room when someone called out her name. "There's someone asking about you, and Mrs. Howe sent me to find you."

Quickly putting the last of the clothes into clean water, she wiped her hands on her apron and rushed to answer the summons. She found Edgar in the administrator's office.

Sally was afraid because she thought he might have come to report her after finding her in the corridor

"There you are," Mrs. Howe had a pleasant smile on her face, which surprised Sally. "Mr. Gillen has been asking about you, as he mentioned that he needed someone to read to his aunt for a couple of hours every afternoon. I told him you could do it."

Sally frowned slightly, "I don't read very well, Mrs. Howe."

"That's no problem," Edgar smiled, and she wanted to run away. There was something in his eyes that made her face turn red and her heart beat faster. It seemed as if Mr. Gillen was giving her romantic looks, but she shook herself inwardly. Men like Edgar Gillen, who were clearly wealthy and very handsome, didn't have time to gaze romantically at paupers and shabbily dressed women like her. The kind of women who would catch his eye were most likely those society ladies who primped and dressed in the latest fashions, smelled of rose water perfumes, and wore expensive jewellery. She forced herself to pay attention to what he was saying. "Aunt Matilda can't understand complex books. I'll buy you some simple literature that you can read to her."

"But-"

"Of course, I will pay you per session. Mrs. Howe tells me that you need the money because you are taking care of your mother. I promise that it won't be hard reading, and your pleasant voice will make a great difference to my poor aunt," he looked at her with something like a desperate plea in his eyes.

Sally sighed inwardly, knowing that she couldn't turn down the offer. It was true that she really needed the money, because things were changing at the institution. She'd overheard her colleagues talking about a new administrator who was here to streamline things. The inpatient fees were set to go up in a few weeks' time. Sally knew that if she couldn't continue paying for the small room she and her charges lived in, they would be forced to take beds in one of the dormitories where there was no privacy. Even though Mrs. Howe had been of much assistance to them in the past, no one knew what the new administration would come up with. She had to have a way of defending her cause if need be, and young as she was, she understood that money was an important factor in such instances.

"Miss Cotton?" Edgar leaned forward and looked into her eyes, "What do you say?"

"As long as they are simple books, then I can do it," she said.

"Good. Now why don't you come with me so I can introduce you to Aunt Matilda."

Aunt Matilda turned out to be a woman in her early seventies, and Sally quickly realized that the woman was very ill. Her skin was white, and Sally could see the coloured veins through it. She looked very frail, and her breathing was laboured. The young woman wondered if the woman would be alive long enough to even get her first reading session, but what touched her most was the way Edgar treated his aunt. As he introduced her, he moved to the head of the bed and gently kissed his aunt's forehead. "Aunt Matilda, I brought someone to meet you," he said in a very soft and tender voice.

"Who?" The woman's voice was raspy.

"Her name is Salome Cotton, and she will be reading to you every day in the afternoon before you take your nap."

Aunt Matilda said something which Sally didn't quite catch, but Edgar smiled as he pointed at the other woman in the room.

"This is Miss Catherine Dane, who takes care of my aunt. Miss Dane has been my aunt's companion for many years, and since you and she are close in age, you'll probably end up as good friends. Miss Dane, you've heard me introduce Salome Cotton to Aunt Matilda. Please give her all the assistance she needs." Sally looked into Catherine's eyes and saw something like anger, but she quickly blinked and then smiled.

"It is wonderful to meet you," Catherine gushed. Sally felt that her smile was insincere, but she couldn't say anything, "Miss Matilda will enjoy your company."

"Thank you," Sally mumbled.

Edgar turned to his aunt's caregiver, "Get some fruit and cake for Miss Cotton. She must be hungry."

"No, thank you, sir. I have to go and take care of my mother. It's nearly time for lunch and I have to get the meals from the dining hall. The queues are usually long, and sometimes the food is gone before I get some."

Edgar frowned, "I thought you worked here, so it should be easy for you to get food from the dining hall."

"That I do, but it's still a bit of a struggle," then Sally checked herself, "not that I'm complaining," she said hurriedly, in case Edgar Gillen took it upon himself to mention something to Mrs. Howe. "We are better off than most, but I still have to take care of Aunt Anne and Mrs. Jane. I've been away from them for too long, and they will no doubt be fretting now."

"Very well, then you can carry the fruits and cake to your charges. But make sure that you come back tomorrow to read to my aunt. I'll come by in the morning to bring you the books you need, and it would be nice if you were here to receive them."

"Yes, sir," Sally bowed. She turned to leave, but Edgar called her back.

"Miss Catherine is packing something for you, just give her a few minutes."

Sally found her aunt and Mrs. Jane crying, and she knew they were hungry. They were like little children, for when one started crying, the other immediately joined her.

"Hush, my beauties," she told them patiently as she divided the fruit and cake and handed each one a plate. Catherine had packed some bananas, oranges, and peaches, as well as a large piece of fruit cake.

Aunt Anne and Mrs. Jane loved sweet things, and they were soon eating happily, tears forgotten, and Sally looked at them with love in her heart and a sigh. If only they would get better.

∽

His Gypsy friends were back, and Oliver was happy. He hadn't seen them in years, and when he'd heard the flute playing and recognized the tune, he'd dashed through the forest to the place where they had last camped out.

The colourful caravans were moving around, and there seemed to be organised chaos as each family found a place to pitch. He was careful not to get in the way as he sought Manfrid and Tillie's caravan, which he spotted and raced toward. Then he came to a sudden halt when he saw a strange woman emerge from inside. Manfrid soon followed and then spotted him.

"Oliver, there you are," Manfrid strode towards him. "We haven't seen each other for a long while, and I'm afraid I have bad news. Tillie passed away last summer when we were in Exeter. And then I met this beautiful woman called Edith, and she is now my wife." Edith was much younger than Tillie had been, but Manfrid seemed happy, so Oliver merely waved to her and she raised her hand back.

"Exeter seems a long way off," Oliver looked around at the Gypsies who were setting up camp, waving to one or two people he recognized. Like him, the young men had grown in the past three years and he saw one with his arm around a very pregnant young woman. Time sure flies, and it waits for no man, he thought.

Manfrid nodded, "Our leaders got us some work there, and that's why we haven't been able to come out here. What have you been up to in all this time?"

Oliver smiled, thinking about how life had become a little easier now that he had a trade. Being a metal smith enabled him to earn an honest living instead of stealing like many young people his age were doing. Making trinkets which he sold to the tourists who visited in summer allowed him to meet a lot of new people, and he had learned much about London and other cities of England from whence they came. Like he did every year, he hoped he would find Sally among the tourists, though he knew it was just a dream. He was also saving up so he could travel around the country to all the towns in search of her. He was sure that Sally was somewhere out there, and he wanted to find her.

"I have become quite adept at making little trinkets to sell to the tourists," he told Manfrid. "It's not much, but I get by."

"Then if you don't mind moving away for a few months, I would like you to come with us to London in a few months."

"What's in London?" Oliver's heart started beating faster.

"During winter, we camp on the outskirts of London and take part in the circuses and fairs there. There's good money to be made by a strapping youth like you," Manfrid looked him up and down. "You've grown so much, and your services can be better used out there."

"Let's wait and see what happens then."

In the months that the Gypsies camped in Bristol, Oliver was careful to learn more from Manfrid. Even though he still visited Mr. Cage, he felt that it was important for him to go to London. He might just bump into Sally and then his search would be over.

16

DEEP HEARTBREAK

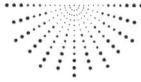

There was great excitement in the air, and Sally found out that the circus was back in town. "This time it's bigger and better than ever," Susan Crane, one of the other nurses' assistants, said. "This year I want those Gypsies to read my fortune." Her eyes glowed. "They might foretell that a rich and handsome man like Edgar Gillen is in my future." The other two girls with her laughed, but Sally paid attention. "We should find time to attend, and especially the night shows. I understand there's so much to see and enjoy."

When Edgar came to visit his aunt, Sally asked him about the circus. They had become good friends, and he smiled at her. "Would you like to go to the circus?"

Sally nodded, but then sighed, "I can't leave my mother and Mrs. Jane without proper supervision."

"Is there someone who can take care of them for a few hours until you return? I could pay them, and then you'll be free."

Edgar arranged for Sally to visit the circus. He got Mrs. Howe to find someone to mind her two charges, and Sally dressed in one of the dresses she had found in the charity crate. It was a simple blue dress, and it brought out the sparkle in her eyes. Edgar knew that she looked like a little girl, but he was still happy to hold her hand as they walked around the circus.

"I've never seen so many beautiful things," she said as she stared at the colourful displays all around her. "But I have to go back to the hospital. Mrs. Howe said we should return quickly." He had indulged her and bought her candy, cakes, pies, and fruit from the vendors, and she knew that for the next three days they wouldn't have to eat the food from the kitchen.

"Did you have a nice time?" Edgar asked. He had bought her a pretty basket to carry all that he had bought her, and he carried it for her.

"Yes, and I hope they will be here again next year."

"They come back every couple years or so," he said, leading her back to his carriage.

When they were headed back to the carriage, Sally thought she saw someone who looked very familiar, but he was dressed in Gypsy clothes. The brief glimpse she got of his face made her heart beat faster.

"What is it?" Edgar asked with concern when he saw how pale she was.

"I thought I saw someone that I know," she whispered. The person she had seen looked so much like Oliver would have after many years. Then she shook her head, "I must be mistaken."

"Who did you think you had seen?"

"One of my cousins who lives in Bristol." She didn't know why she lied to Edgar, but she didn't think that he needed to know about Oliver and her strong feelings for him. "But the person I saw was wearing Gypsy clothes, and my cousin isn't one of them."

"You sound like you're missing your family."

Sally bit her lower lip, "That is my father's side of the family, but they are distant relatives. I just wish I could visit Bristol to see them."

"Why don't you go and see them?"

Sally turned to stare at Edgar. "First, I don't have the money to go to Bristol, and I can't leave my mother and Mrs. Jane for so many days."

Edgar laughed softly, "You are such a simple girl, my Sally. Anything can be arranged as long as money is involved. I know that Mrs. Howe would do anything I asked of her, and if you want to go and visit your father's distant relatives, then I can make it possible. Besides, with trains these days, it will only take you a few hours to get there, greet your relatives, and then get back on the train to return. You don't have to spend the night in Bristol, and Mrs. Howe will be most agreeable," he said confidently.

"Thank you," Sally gave him a glowing smile, and the gentleman wished he could kiss her pretty lips, though she was but a child. He sighed inwardly, knowing that he needed to be patient and wait for her to grow up. From the moment he had set his eyes on her, he'd yearned for her, but she was only fifteen. Showing any kind of romantic attention toward her wouldn't be received well in his circles, so he would wait until she turned eighteen, after which he fully intended to make her his wife.

"Don't mention it. I will make the necessary arrangements. You just tell me when you're ready to go to Bristol."

～

Edgar had kept his promise and made arrangements for Sally to visit Bristol. He still thought she was going to see her father's distant relative because she hadn't wanted to tell him that her intention was to find Oliver. He had gone above and beyond a simple favour and even gotten her someone to take care of her aunt and Mrs. Jane for the two days that she expected to be away. And not only that, after getting her a train ticket, he had arranged for conveyance from the station in Bristol to the manor and then back whenever she was ready. A simple telegram to a friend had everything arranged.

There was a carriage waiting for her as soon as she stepped off the train, and the driver met her. He'd clearly been watching out for her, because as soon as she stood on the platform, he approached her. Once she had identified herself, he escorted her to his old but very clean carriage.

"You must be someone really special to Mr. Gillen," the old driver told her as he helped her into the carriage.

"Why?"

"My employer got a telegram requesting urgent conveyance to the Winchester Manor, and not only that, my instructions are that I am to wait for you and do everything you ask."

"That is very kind of you." Sally tried to give him a tip when they got close to the manor, but he shook his head.

"I wouldn't feel right taking a penny from you when I have been paid more than I usually make on such a journey. Just finish your business at the manor, and I'll be waiting to take you to the station for your train back to London."

"I don't want anyone to know who I am, so would you please wait for me down the road?" The man gave her an odd look but followed her instructions. She just hoped he wouldn't report back to Edgar about her unusual request.

Seeing the house where her aunt had worked for nearly four years brought back sad memories for Sally. She was very sure that none of the people living in the large manor could remember her, because she had left when she was just a small child. Nine years was a long time, and she prayed that she would be successful in her quest.

Many thoughts crossed through her mind as she walked up to the front door and knocked. She wondered if Oliver would recognize her, and if the man in the dungeon was still alive. Hurried footsteps came to the door. which was flung open.

"Thank goodness you've arrived," a stressed-out-looking middle-aged woman said. "I thought you would be coming tomorrow, but I'm glad to see you. Come, we don't have time to waste. Miss Maeve is getting engaged today, and there is much to do."

Sally allowed herself to be dragged through the large living room, where she saw three maids busy dusting and rearranging the furniture. This was the part of the house that she'd never entered as a small child, and she was quite impressed.

The room was beautifully adorned with a large crystal chandelier in the centre. The walls had been draped in soft lilac sheers, and a small stage had been set up with two seats placed on it. These were covered in rich purple cloth. It was a very large room that could comfortably hold about fifty people. The overall feeling that Sally had as they quickly passed through the living room was that no expense had been spared when it came to the decor. There were flowers everywhere, bright yellow, white, and red ones. She longed to see what Maeve looked like, and she imagined that her dress would most probably be out of this world.

If Mrs. Winchester had splurged on the decor, she would have put even more into her daughter's adornments.

"Come," the woman pulled her down the hallway and into the kitchen. In all the years that Sally had been in this home, she'd never seen the kitchen so busy.

There were three cooks, each doing various tasks. "Help Andrew over there," the woman pointed, "He's baking pies and scones."

Sally wanted to tell the woman that she wasn't here to work but she decided to keep silent. Perhaps she would be able to find out more about Oliver. She moved closer to Andrew and gave him a brief smile. "My name is Salome."

"No time for chatting," the woman said as she clapped her fat hands. "We have to get everything ready for the engagement of the year. Mrs. Winchester expects everything to be done by the time Miss Maeve's betrothed arrives, and that's in about two hours."

The last time Sally had been in this kitchen was on the day that Mr. Winchester had attacked her aunt. Not much had changed except those who now worked in it, but she felt very strange stepping into the one place she'd never expected to return to. Now that she had grown up and been out in the world, she finally understood what the man had tried to do. He would have defiled her aunt if Tubby hadn't come to the rescue. Tubby, that dear cat! Sally knew that cats didn't live very long, and she thought about the feline that had saved hers and Oliver's lives many times.

She was also curious about Mr. Winchester and wondered if he was still alive. Her eyes went to the large grate, and she shuddered, recalling how the man had fallen face down into the boiling cauldron.

"There is something very odd about that fellow," Andrew was saying.

"What fellow?" Sally picked up an apron and quickly tied it around her waist.

"The prospective groom."

"Oh?" Sally's interest was piqued. "Why would you say that?"

"He has shifty eyes, and even though Mrs. Winchester says he's a very wealthy man,there's something very odd about him."

"I haven't met him since I've only arrived. Have you been here for long?"

"One year now, and let me tell you, this is trouble waiting to happen."

"If they are in love, then that's all that should count, don't you think?" But even as Sally spoke out in defence of Maeve, she remembered how the girl and her brother had tormented Oliver. Perhaps she had changed.

Andrew snorted, "There's nothing like love between those two." He looked around then lowered his head. "I hear that the Winchesters have run out of money, so they are looking for a wealthy husband for Maeve to bail them out. This is a marriage with no love."

Sally was silent for a brief moment. She'd never interacted with Maeve in the past, but she could recall how she and Kent had made life very unpleasant for Oliver.

"Is Miss Maeve an only child?" She was fishing for information and used a roundabout way.

"No, she has one brother, a very unpleasant and arrogant fellow," he looked at her, "You better stay hidden in the kitchen all the time."

"Why?"

"Because the fellow has a roving , even though he is supposedly engaged to be married to some socialite in London. He troubles the other maids and Mrs. Rowan, the housekeeper, has had to employ young men to clean the bed chambers. Nasty fellow, that one," Andrew shuddered. "And as mean as a viper. Stay hidden is my advice, or you'll soon find yourself fighting to save your virtue from his roaming hands."

Sally longed to ask about Oliver, but Mrs. Rowan returned to the kitchen, and all chatting ceased.

It was a lavish affair, and Sally worked herself to the bone. She didn't plan on being here the whole day, and in the middle of the afternoon, she approached Mrs. Rowan.

"May I have my wages for today, Ma'am?"

"Why? Don't you like working here?"

"It's too much work, and besides I was told that I was coming to take care of a seven-year-old child and be the governess."

Mrs. Rowan gave her an odd look. "There's no child in this house. There hasn't been one for ages. I've worked here for eight years now, and the only children, who are now adults, are Miss Maeve and Master Kent. I understand the

Winchesters had a third child, but he died nine years ago, poor child."

Sally felt like her heart was being crushed. Oliver had died nine years ago.

"What happened to him?"

The middle-aged woman shrugged. "He was ill or something. It was months before I came here, so I really don't know."

"My wages, please," Sally whispered.

"Here," the woman gave her a few pennies. Sally didn't want to argue. "You might want to use the back door, since the guests have started arriving, and Mrs. Winchester will take exception to a maid traipsing through the living room."

"Thank you."

She didn't want darkness to find her in the vicinity of the manor, for then she would be forced to ask for a place to spend the night. She practically ran out of the kitchen, down the driveway, and out to the main road where she found the carriage waiting for her.

"Took you long enough," the man said, but in a cheery voice. "For a moment I thought you would be spending the night in that place," he shuddered. "Did you find your kin?"

"No, sir," she answered sadly, fighting back her tears. "I was told he died nine years ago, which was around the time my mother and I left this place." She sniffled. "Thank you for waiting for me."

"Will you be spending a night in Bristol?"

"No, sir. If I could catch a night train back to London, I will be most grateful."

"Aye, there are trains running through at all hours of the day, and it shouldn't be difficult to catch the London one. And I'm sorry for your loss, Miss."

"You're a very kind man."

Oliver was dead, and she had no desire to stay in Potter's Cove for a single moment longer than was necessary.

~

Oliver peered through the trees to see if the coast was clear. He had brought some food for the man in the dungeon, but more than that, he had clippers to finish cutting the shackles. He had forged them himself with the help of Manfrid, who gave him a stern warning as they were working on the tools.

"I hope you have no intentions of breaking and entering people's homes with those tools. For that would then mean that I'm abating a criminal."

"No, sir," he said. "These are to cut traps after I set them. Once I catch animals, it sometimes becomes very difficult to separate them from the , and the last thing my customers want is to buy animals whose limbs have been mangled by the traps. These clippers will help me make a neat job of it."

Oliver smiled as he approached the house through the woods. He saw a young woman dart from the back and then tear down the driveway as if someone was chasing her. Something about her disturbed him, but he put the thoughts aside as he concentrated on what he had come to do. Mr. Cage needed to be freed, and if Oliver could accomplish it, he would take him to the forest and live with him until the Gypsies were ready to return to Potter's Cove Village. After that, he would ask Manfrid to take them both to London, where he would find work as a metal smith or tinker and support the two of them. It had to be tonight. He must get Mr. Cage out of here. He couldn't understand why he was so attached to the man in the dungeons, even nine years later. Coming to the mansion was always a risk, because he could be spotted, and then there would be trouble.

Some sort of celebration was going on in the house, but that didn't concern him. His purpose was to get Mr. Cage free. No matter how many times Oliver asked the man to tell him his name, he would only shake his head and turn away.

When he was sure there was no one around to see him, he slipped into the abandoned well at the corner of the compound. He'd found out that this was one of the hidden passages in the dungeon. It surprised him that no one in the manor apart from him and Sally had known about whoever was in the dungeon.

He often wondered about whoever had put the man in the dungeon for this long. So many times, he'd wanted to tell Manfrid about it, but he would always remember the promise he had made.

"Never let anyone know that you have found me."

"But I don't like seeing you locked up in this dungeon."

"One day you'll understand. If anything, being down here is what keeps me safe. So keep silent until the day I will tell you to speak up."

Oliver shook his head as he crawled through the tunnel. Just as he was about to enter the one that held the prisoner, he heard voices and ran back to hide.

"Make sure there's no one down here," a gruff voice said, "I saw a few of the youngsters running in this direction, and we wouldn't want them to see what they are not supposed to

164

see. I don't want to have to kill anyone but if my hand is forced, I won't hesitate."

Oliver crawled up to the well, climbed up and fled, not once looking back. This was the wrong time for him to have come to try and rescue Mr. Cage. As he scrambled up the well, he thought he heard footsteps coming toward him and he didn't look behind.

∾

Maeve was floating on a cloud as she walked through the room on Cliff's arm. She knew that she looked beautiful, for her mother had done her best to make sure that she outshone all the other young women present. Kent was smiling at her while he spoke to one of the many young women who had attended her engagement party. Kent told her that he was betrothed to a girl who was just sixteen, and so he was waiting for her to turn eighteen so he could introduce her to their parents. Her family was extremely wealthy and influential, two things Kent strove for with all his being.

The one thing that dampened the mood of the day was the fact that her father had refused to leave his bedchamber. For the past nine years, he rarely left his rooms, and his valet did everything for him. Maeve wanted him to meet Cliff because she felt that the two of them would get along very nicely, but at least she had Kent, who was now the man of the house.

"Are you happy, my darling?" Cliff only had eyes for her, and she basked in his loving gaze.

"Very much so," she said breathlessly.

"I'm glad to hear it," Cliff looked around. "If I didn't respect you so much, I would ask you to elope to Gretna Green with me, so we don't have to wait for the wedding. I don't know how long I'm going to be able to continue holding on to my sanity."

"Why?" She gave him a coy look.

"Because I am in love with you and can't wait for you to be my wife." He stopped and pulled her aside, "Why don't we elope?"

"My mother would never forgive me," Maeve said, even though the idea really appealed to her. "We have only three months until our wedding."

"Darling, that is too long for me to wait." He pouted. "Or don't you want to marry me? Why do I get the feeling that you're only leading me on and have no intentions of marrying me?"

"No, please don't say that," Maeve murmured desperately. She couldn't risk Cliff changing his mind about marrying her. She was the envy of her peers, and she could see their covetous looks as they watched her and Cliff. What's more, he'd given Kent a great deal of money to prepare for this engagement party, and everyone was talking about how lavish and wonderful it was.

"We could elope and then when we return, we can have a big reception for your family and friends. My darling, please don't keep me waiting, for I don't know if I can survive without you."

Maeve thought for a brief moment, and then nodded. "All right, I'll elope with you."

"Do you really mean that?" Cliff looked happy once again, and Maeve pushed away all the warnings at the back of her mind.

"Yes. I love you and want to do what you want. My desire is to make you happy."

"What about your mother?"

"If we get Kent on our side, he will know how to handle my mother. I think Kent likes you very much, and all he wants is for me to be happy. So when can we leave for Gretna Green?"

"Tonight, after the engagement party," he whispered, and her heart started pounding in great anticipation. "And then I will take you to Tuscany for a few days on our honeymoon so you can meet my family."

Maeve was very agreeable, because she was yet to meet any of Cliff's family. He'd told her that they lived in Europe, and she could just imagine the envy that would be in everyone's heart when they heard that she had honeymooned in Europe, and beautiful Tuscany of all the places.

"Yes," she repeated, her eyes glowing with love and great expectations.

17

THROUGH THE MIST

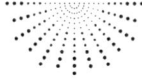

"I feel like I have been on a long journey." Sally looked up sharply and realized that it was Aunt Anne who had spoken those words very clearly. For six years her aunt had only spoken gibberish, distorted words and sentences. "It's like the mist that had clouded my mind has lifted." She looked around her. "I feel like I was in a long dark tunnel but now have burst forth into the light. What is happening to me?" Sally was folding clean laundry and stopped what she was doing to stare at her aunt.

"Aunt Anne?" Sally approached the bed, not quite believing what she was hearing. Aunt Anne sat up slowly, her eyes fixed on Sally.

"I feel as if I should know you," she scratched her face, "Do I know you?" she looked around. "Where am I, and where is my little Sally?" Tears started falling down her cheeks. "What happened to my Sally?"

"Aunt Anne!" Sally sat on the bed and took the distraught woman's hands, "It's me, Sally."

"But you look so different," Anne reached out a hand and touched her face, "Your eyes and hair tell me that it's you, but your face looks grown."

"That's because I'm all grown up now, Aunt Anne. I turned eighteen last week."

"How?" Anne whispered.

Sally looked sad. "Six years ago, you fell and bumped your head and became unconscious. I kept hoping you would wake up, but you didn',t and we had to take you to the hospital. When you regained consciousness, we brought you to this institution. I have been taking care of you and Mrs. Jane for the past six years, Aunt Anne."

"Six years? And who is Mrs. Jane?"

Sally pointed at the other woman, who was sleeping. "We found her here when we came in, and I've been taking care of the two of you ever since."

"Oh, you poor child," Anne looked around her and took in the shabby-but-homely, medium-sized room, "This looks like a room in an inn, and not one in a mental institution.

Sally didn't want her aunt to see the guilty look on her face, so she went back to the laundry that she'd been folding. Yes, their room was much bigger and better furnished than the previous one, and it was all because of Edgar. Once the new administration was in place, they had insisted on everyone, including staff, paying hefty fees for their rooms.

After returning from her unsuccessful trip to Bristol, Sally had continued to read to Edgar's aunt, though not for long, because Miss Matilda had passed away just a few days later. Thinking that was going to be the last time she would see Edgar, Sally had been surprised when one of her colleagues had brought him to their previous room. Sally had been embarrassed at how dark and unpleasant it was, and she stood at the door, not willing to let him in.

"You live in this hovel?" He pushed her aside and none too gently, "Why didn't you tell me?"

"I'm sorry," she felt the need to say.

"Oh, Salome, my dearest," he approached her and held her shoulders, "You beautiful girl, you don't have to live like this. I can give you anything you need and even more."

"Why?"

"Because you're very special to me. I fell in love with you the first day I saw you, but I feel very guilty." He looked down at her and she felt something fluttering within her heart. He was a very handsome man. "How old are you, Salome?"

"Fifteen," she said, wishing he would go away, because he was making her feel funny.

"Why, you're but a babe!" He dropped his hands. "I thought you were seventeen or eighteen, for then I would ask for your hand in marriage."

"What?" Of all that she was expecting him to say, marriage was the last thing. "Marry me? But you don't know me at all. How old are you?" She blurted out, and then felt her face flaming at what might be construed as insolence. "I'm sorry," she mumbled.

"Salome, I'm thirty years old but I can't help how I feel. Yet you're so young." He stepped out of the room, "But I'm a patient man and I can wait for you. Three years isn't a long time to wait, and as soon as you turn eighteen, we shall be married."

"Mr. Gillen-."

"Seeing as we're all but engaged, why don't you call me Edgar?" He looked at her and she felt her hands sweating. "Promise me that you

won't let any other lout steal your heart from me." He grabbed her shoulders and shook her, an earnest and almost desperate look in his eyes, "Promise me."

Just to get him to stop shaking her, Sally nodded. She felt like he was pushing her, but she didn't want him to continue shaking her.

"Good!" He pulled out an old ring with a faded ruby from his pocket and pushed it onto her finger. She tried to resist, but his hands were stronger. "This belonged to Aunt Matilda, and I know she would have wanted you to have it. Now everyone will know that you belong to me and no one else."

Sally gulped, wanting to pull the ring off her finger, but she didn't want him to be offended.

"And now that we have that out of the way, I'll have to see to alternative boarding arrangements for you," and he didn't wait for her to say anything else but walked away.

"Sally? Sally!" Her aunt's voice brought her back to the present. "Come here," the firm tone brooked no nonsense, and Sally put the folded laundry away. "Tell me that you didn't do something terrible to get us these quarters." Sally swallowed, "Salome, speak at once. You may be eighteen, but I can still take you over my knee." Sally raised a shaking hand to tuck a loose strand of hair behind her ear. Anne exclaimed, "What is that?"She grabbed Sally's hand before she could hide the hideous ring, "What did you do, Sally?"

"I got engaged," she whispered hoarsely as she tried to avoid her aunt's eyes for fear of what she would see. "His name is Edgar Gillen."

"Sally, what did I tell you about men and getting close to them? Have you been to his house?"

"No, ma'am."

"Where and how did you meet?" Aunt Anne asked. Sally quickly told her, then fell silent.

"Sally, I know you thought you were doing all this for me and Mrs. Jane over there, but your virtue should never be compromised. Didn't you listen when I told you that nothing is ever for free? This man wants something from you, and I pray that you haven't been foolish enough to give it to him."

Sally knew what her aunt was referring to, and she shook her head, "No, Aunt Anne, Edgar has been the perfect gentleman all through, and helped me take care of you."

"Are you sure that the man hasn't put his hands on you?" Anne peered at her face. "Tell me, Sally, be honest with me."

"No, ma'am, he hasn't," Sally said in a breathless voice, but her aunt didn't seem quite convinced of the fact. Sally felt shame welling up within her breast, because she had really been tempted to act improperly once.

That was the time three years ago that she had returned from Bristol. Her heart was in pain and anguish after finding out that Oliver was dead. When she arrived back in London, Edgar had been waiting at the station for her because she'd sent him a telegram to let him know that she was on her way back. She had been weeping at having lost Oliver and was very confused. She told him that her kin had died nine years ago. When Edgar suggested they go to his house so she could spend the night there, she hadn't put up any resistance.

"The woman who is taking care of your mother and the other woman will be there until tomorrow, so there's no need for you to get back to Bedlam tonight. Besides, it's very late, and I know that the administration usually frowns upon residents returning at this ungodly hour. Mrs. Howe would be most upset with you. Spend the night at my house and first thing in the morning, I'll take you back to your mother."

The distraught girl had needed to be comforted, and he'd put his arms around her, whispering words of love in her young ears.

The only thing that had stopped her from letting him have his way with her was seeing Catherine Dane at the house. A look of annoyance had fleetingly passed over Edgar's face.

"What are you doing here?" he'd barked at Catherine.

"I came to see you." The woman was crying, and something about her anguish touched Sally. That's when she realized Catherine was in love with Edgar. There was something happening between them, for Edgar was harsh, almost to the point of being brutal.

"Take me to the hospital," Sally had insisted, and when Edgar hesitated, she rushed out of the house. He'd reluctantly driven her back, and once he was sure she was inside, had driven away without a backward glance.

"Salome," Aunt Anne shook her, "If I find that you have compromised your virtue, I will be so disappointed, it will break my heart." Tears coursed down her pale cheeks.

"I promise," Sally knelt before her aunt," I have never compromised my virtue, Aunt Anne." She laid her head on her aunt's lap and wept. Anne gently stroked her hair.

"It's all right, I believe you. But I remember that you once told me very firmly and confidently that you would never marry anyone but Oliver."

"Oliver is dead." She told her aunt everything that had happened three years ago when she had visited Bristol, and also about Maeve's engagement party that she'd chanced upon.

"Well, now that I'm better, we'll go to Bristol." Anne frowned. Edgar Gillen had taken advantage of an innocent and desperate girl, but now that she was well, she was back in charge of Sally's life. "The only way that I will let you marry another man and give yourself to him is if we get to Bristol and see Oliver's grave. Otherwise your so-called betrothed man will have to wait."

"Yes, Aunt Anne." Sally felt as if a load had rolled off her back. Her aunt was back to her normal self and would take care of the daunting Edgar. For three years, he'd done everything for them because he hoped to marry her, and even though she didn't love him, she'd felt indebted to him. Aunt Anne and her straightforwardness would soon set things right.

"Now we have to think about getting out of this place."

"I have been working and saving money," Sally said. "It isn't that much, but it will help us start somewhere." Then she looked at Mrs. Jane. "But I don't want to leave Mrs. Jane alone."

"How is it that you came to be taking care of her as well?"

"When we first got here, Mrs. Jane was hiding in the room that was given to us then. It was much smaller than this. Mrs. Howe wanted to send her away, but there's just something about her that made me want to take care of her. And she has been a good companion for you."

Anne pulled her niece closer. "Sally, I'm so sorry that you lost your childhood and had to grow up so fast. I can't ever repay you for the care you have shown me when I wasn't quite myself. But now I am all right and will continue taking care of you."

"I'm just so happy that you're well again, Aunt Anne."

"And just in time," she grinned. "For my little lamb might have been married to a man I might not approve of, just to save me."

For sure, Aunt Anne didn't like Edgar Gillen when she finally met him, but she had urged Sally not to let him know that she was well. All Sally did was to take Mrs. Jane and Aunt Anne to the small park at the front of the hospital. When Edgar arrived to see her like he did every day, she had introduced him, even though he'd never shown any interest before.

"I'm sorry that my aunt and Mrs. Jane won't recognize you, but I wanted you to meet them properly. The other times you have come to see me, they were asleep."

"I hope they will like living in my house when you and I get married," he said, holding her hand, and she pretended to be wiping the drool off Aunt Anne's mouth and pulled away. When they went back to their room, Aunt Anne expressed her displeasure.

"Why, that man is nearly twice your age, Sally. Why would he want to marry you, unless he has some sinister motives in mind?"

"I don't know, but at least he never bothered me nor tried to get me to compromise my virtue."

"I'll just say that I'm grateful to the man for ensuring that you were well taken care of and protected while you were here. Now we have to think of leaving."

"We can't leave Mrs. Jane behind," Sally said in a firm voice. "Why don't we stay here until I can make some more money so we can get a good cottage somewhere to live in."

"But for how long?"

"Maybe another year, Aunt Anne. It will also prevent Mr. Gillen from insisting on getting married. The moment we let him know that you're well and we walk out of here, he will follow us and compel me to marry him."

"A year is a long time. What will I be doing in all that time?"

"You could begin acting as if you're getting lucid but then keep reverting to insanity. In that way when we finally declare that you're well and want to leave, no one will be the wiser. I pray that Mrs. Jane will also get better. She's been acting differently for a few weeks now, and I believe she is also on the road to recovery."

"You are a wonder, child."

"Not really, just blessed to have had the opportunity of taking care of you and Mrs. Jane."

18

FOLLOWING A DREAM

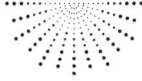

"Salome! Salome, where are you girl?"

Sally rushed out of the laundry room and stopped when she saw Mrs. Howe, who looked flustered.

"You called for me, ma'am."

"Yes. There's a young man asking about someone called Claire Burnham but we have no patient here by that name. However, from the description he gave and the year she supposedly got admitted here, it's clear that he's talking about Mrs. Jane. Do you know if her other name is Claire?"

Sally shook her head, wiping her wet hands on the apron. "I took my mother and Mrs. Jane out to the yard to bask. Perhaps if the visitor could see her, he might tell us if she's the person he seeks."

"Very well, go and get them ready, and I'll bring him to the back to meet Mrs. Jane."

The moment the smartly dressed man came into view, Sally heard her aunt gasp, and she turned to look at her, but she didn't address her because they still hadn't let Mrs. Howe know that Anne was healed.

"This will be the gentleman who is asking about Claire Burnham. I'll leave you to it then, for I have work to do back in the office," Mrs. Howe said and walked away.

That's when Sally turned to her aunt. "Aunt Anne are you alright? Do you know this man?"

"No," Anne seemed to have a difficult time catching her breath and Sally feared that she might swoon. She was surprised to see that the visitor could also not help himself from staring at Aunt Anne.

"Who are you?" Sally demanded before even greeting the man.

"Salome," Aunt Anne hissed.

"I'm sorry," she had the grace to feel ashamed, but she'd never seen her aunt so affected by the sight of a man before, not in all the time that they had lived back in Bristol or even here in London.

"My name is Casper Trent, and I came to look for Mrs. Claire Burnham. Do you know her?" Sally shook her head. "I understand you are taking care of two patients."

"Yes, this is my Aunt Anne and-"

"Casper?" Sally and Anne turned when they heard Mrs. Jane's voice, "Is that really you?" To their surprise, she rushed into his arms. It was clearly an emotional moment for them, and when it had passed, she held his hand and led him to the seat. "This is Casper," she said happily. "And my name is Claire Burnham, not Jane," she winked at Sally.

"Mrs. Burnham, I am so happy to see you." Casper wiped the tears from her eyes. "For twenty years I've prayed for this day, and that I would find you alive."

"Where did you go?"

Casper sighed and then looked at Sally and Anne, "Who are these people?" he asked.

"This is Sally, and she's been taking very good care of me." Sally couldn't believe that the woman she had thought of as being severely mentally retarded was very lucid and was even aware that Sally had been taking care of her."

"How?" she managed to ask.

Claire Burnham gave her a sweet smile. "I was really ill for many years before you and your aunt came here. I was starting to get better when I noticed that some of the male orderlies were being very improper towards some female patients. So, I deliberately made myself as unpleasant and filthy as I could so none of them would harm me. But then you came, and I knew I couldn't let you know I was well. You see, Casper was gone, and I knew that my husband and son were dead. Since I had nowhere to go, I decided that I would continue to pretend to be mentally deranged so I could be safe. I was ready to live here for the rest of my life."

"And Aunt Anne got better two months ago, but we didn't want to leave you in here," Sally said, and they all laughed.

Claire turned to Casper, "Where did you go after you brought me here?"

He grimaced, "For the sake of your new friends let me start at the beginning."

Casper was ten years old when his father died, and he started working as Mr. Oscar Burnham's valet. When he turned fifteen, Mr.

Burnham married Claire and brought her home. Then her sister Marie, who was married to a worthless fellow called Grant, came to live with them. Claire loved her older sister and wanted to do all she could for her and her family, but she had no idea that she was harbouring a viper in her bosom. At the time, Claire was expecting a child, and when her son was born, she named him Oliver. But she had had a long labour and she became very confused. Marie tried to convince her brother-in-law to get Claire committed to an asylum, but Oscar refused. He knew that his sister-in-law was out for trouble, so he asked Casper to take Claire to London, and he would join them.

On the night they were supposed to leave, Marie took little Oliver away and threatened to kill him if Claire didn't leave. Casper saw trouble and managed to get Claire out of the house and to London. He didn't want any harm coming to the poor woman, so he took her to Bedlam Mental Hospital, hoping she would get better. He would visit her every day, but one day as he was coming to see her, he was arrested and charged with murder. Then he was sentenced to be taken to the colonies. The original plan was to take him to Australia, but he ended up on a ship to America instead.

"I had to find work because I wanted to pay for a better room for you, Mrs. Burnham. I believed you would get well, and that Mr. Oscar would find a way of getting your son back, and then they would join us here in London." He looked sad. "Once I had admitted you here, I even went to back Bristol, but I heard that Mr. Oscar had been killed by bandits, and Oliver too. So, I came back here, and one day I was falsely accused of being part of a gang that had robbed some wealthy man. It was God's grace that I wasn't hanged. Instead I was banished to Australia. Due to a mix up in some documents, I was put on a ship to America."

The three women gasped.

"Once there, the man who was supposed to be my master rejected me because I was very ill. The journey across the sea was terrible, and a number of people died. I was very lonely, and I wandered the streets of New York till an old man took pity on me. He told me about the west and how he'd heard that people were finding gold, silver, and precious stones in the hills. He asked me to cast my lot in with him. I had nothing, but I promised to be his servant." Casper fell silent and the women waited, not taking their eyes off him.

"We ended up in Birchwood, Oregon, and the first few years were terrible. We were barely eking out a living, and Old Stone, my master, nearly died of a broken heart. For fifteen years, we had done all we could, but nothing happened. I had to work as a cowhand just so we could eat." He smiled. "But two years ago, the Lord remembered us, and we struck gold."

The three women clapped happily.

"Yes, we found a vein of gold that was so rich that overnight we became very wealthy. Mr. Stone wanted us to buy a ranch and run it together, but my heart has always been set on returning back home and making sure you were fine. So, I helped him to buy a hundred acres of land and some steers, and then for about a year and a half, helped him to establish himself. Lucky for me, Mr. Stone met a lovely widow who has three sons, and they got married. Once I was sure they weren't just after his money and that he would be all right, I decided to come back home. My intention was that I would come and find you, Mrs. Burnham. Then I would help you get back what is rightfully yours from your wicked sister."

"Oh, Casper, I gave up years ago. I can't go back to Bristol, because my Oscar is no more." She started crying. "Oliver would be about twenty-one now. If only my sister and her husband hadn't done that to us."

"Mrs. Oscar tried to warn you that the Winchesters were up to no good."

"Wait," Anne broke in, giving Sally an odd look. "You wouldn't perhaps be talking about Mr. Grant and Mrs. Marie Winchester, would you?"

"Yes, that's them." Casper sounded excited, "Do you know them?"

Anne shifted uncomfortably, "Nearly twelve years ago, I worked as their cook. Their youngest son, who was three years older than Sally, was named Oliver."

Claire had a hand to her lips. "That was my son, I'm sure of it. Please tell me he was alive when you left."

Anne looked at Sally and nodded slightly. "Sally went back three years ago and was told that Oliver had died years back."

Claire crumpled, and Casper held her close as she sobbed, "What about any news of Mr. Oscar? While you lived there, did you ever hear about him?"

Anne and Sally shook their heads, "No, one ever mentioned such a person," Anne said. "So just as Mr. Trent said, he must have been killed by bandits."

"The name is Casper." He smiled at Anne, and she blushed. That's when Sally realised that these two were attracted to each other. "Please call me Casper."

"Thank you."

"Now that we have the full story, I need to get Mrs. Claire out of here." He looked at Anne and Sally. "Do you have somewhere to go?"

"Casper," Claire wiped her eyes, "you can't leave Anne and Sally here. They have taken care of me for the past six years, and even after Anne got well, they refused to leave me alone. They are now my family, and where I go, they will go too."

"Very well then, what I need to do is to get the two of you examined by a doctor and to be declared well enough to be discharged. When I arrived a week ago, I purchased a town house right here in London because I was hoping you would still be alive so you would come and live with me. It's a big house, and we can all live there."

"You don't have to do that," Anne said. "Now that you're here, Sally and I can find our own way."

"That will never happen," Claire said forcefully. "Besides, I have become attached to you, and we can be companions for the rest of our lives. What's more, it is very clear that you and Casper seem well suited to each other."

"But there is still one problem we have," Anne said when Claire had finally convinced her that they should live together.

"What's that?"

"My niece here got engaged to a much older man, and I believe that he took advantage of the desperation we were in to convince her to be his wife. Claire and I have met the man, and while he looks like a gentleman, I don't want my Sally to be his wife. He won't make her happy." Claire was nodding as Anne said this.

"Then we shall have to find a way of getting this Edgar person to change his mind, won't we?"

～

Casper couldn't believe that he was back home in England, and not as a pauper but as a very wealthy man. As he sat in his house and waited for his cook to prepare dinner, he rang the small bell to summon his valet.

Henry Dickens was a much older man, but he came with excellent references from the family of his previous employer, a gentleman who had passed away just a few months ago.

"You summoned me, sir?"

"Dickens, would you please sit down? I need to pick your brain."

"Very well, sir." The man sat on the opposite seat.

"Have you heard of a man called Edgar Gillen?"

"I believe I have, sir. My former master was his good friend. Is there a problem with Mr. Gillen, sir?"

"What kind of a man is he?"

Dickens tilted his head to the side as if lost in thought. "The man always struck me as being an odd fellow, but I could be biased."

"Why would you say that?"

"My cousin was his aunt's companion for many years. She joined the household when she was sixteen, and I suspected that he took advantage of her, if you know what I mean." He cleared his throat. "Whenever I asked Kate, my cousin, she always denied it. Mrs. Matilda Gower was good to her, and she seemed to enjoy her work."

"What happened to your cousin?"

"When Mrs. Gower died three years ago, Kate continued to live in the house. I haven't seen her in a long time, so I can't tell you for sure how she is faring on right now."

"Is there a way that you can bring your cousin to see me?"

"I could try. But why are you so interested in Mr. Edgar?"

"Let's just speak to your cousin, and then I will tell you what is going on."

Two days later, Dickens brought his cousin to see Casper. "This is my cousin Kate and as you can see…" Dickens was shaking his head.

"You have twins?" Casper looked down at the two boys with identical faces who looked to be two years old.

"Yes, sir," Kate whispered huskily.

"Are you all right?"

"Kate, can you tell Mr. Trent everything that you shared with me?"

"Yes, I will."

❧

"I'm sorry, Edgar. I can't marry you." Sally held out his ring, which he refused to take back. They had all been discharged after the doctor pronounced the two women to be well, and Casper took them to his house. He had then sent a message to Edgar, and the man had shown up, not suspecting that things were about to change for him.

"I paid for your board for three years," he hissed. "I looked after you and these two women, and now you tell me that you won't marry me? What effrontery. You'll pay me for all my wasted time, or I'll have you thrown into the Debtors' Prison until you pay every last farthing that you owe me. Ungrateful creatures, all of you," he glared at them with thinly disguised contempt in his eyes.

Sally felt her face flaming, and she was glad that she wasn't getting married to this nasty man. He was showing her another side of him. "But-"

"Let me, "Casper looked at Edgar. "Sir, first you're too old for this young girl, and secondly, I know that another woman bore your two children." Edgar's face turned white as Sally stared at Casper in disbelief.

"Sally's aunt told me all about your so-called benevolence, which clearly came with a lot of demands. I had my people do some investigation. Will you deny knowing Miss Catherine Dane now? She is the mother of your two children. I also know that you have put her up in a small cottage so you can hide her from society, even though your aunt made provision for the young woman to live in her house for the rest of her life."

"What?" Sally turned accusing eyes to Edgar, "How could you be so cruel, and to your own flesh and blood?" She grabbed his hand and pressed his ring in it. "I never want to see you again."

"My money-"

"I'll settle everything Sally and her aunt may or may not owe you, and I will even add interest at the current market prices. I suggest that you do the right thing by Miss Dane, and marry the mother of your children. You're a respectable man, and I know you guard your reputation fiercely. Just imagine if word were to get out that you wanted to molest an underage girl, and that you had turned away from your own children. What's more, Miss Dane's cousin is my valet, and he told me something very interesting about how you started taking advantage of her when she was only sixteen."

"That's a lie," Edgar paled.

"But who will believe your story?" Casper asked, knowing that he had the man well and truly cornered. "That young woman was your aunt's companion for many years and lived under your roof. Now it turns out that she bore twins for you, who I'm waiting to hear you deny."

"Did she say they were my children?"

"She didn't have to say it. They look like you, and it's a good thing that they are both boys. I only have to get the word out to a few people, and you will be in a lot of trouble, Mr. Gillen. So I suggest that you do the right thing and release Sally and her aunt from any indebtedness to you. But don't worry, I will settle the whole amount you spent on them. I'm glad that this girl is very wise." Casper pointed to Sally. "She kept a tally of every single farthing you gave her, so what I will do is mark it up by twenty percent. Is that agreeable to you?"

"Yes."

"And do you promise to do the right thing by Miss Dane?"

"I'll do that," Edgar's shoulders dropped, and Sally felt a little sorry for him. "And I promise that I will marry Catherine and give my sons a name."

"I will be watching to see that you treat her with respect and care. If it ever gets to my ears that you've made that young woman's life miserable, London will not contain you, Mr. Gillen."

"I'm an honourable man, and I will stand by my word," he said. He then turned to Sally, "I'm very sorry."

"My solicitor will be in touch with you to sort out the issue of what is owed to you. And Mr. Gillen, thank you for what you did for Sally and Anne, and also Mrs. Burnham."

Edgar nodded and left without saying another word.

Sally felt like a huge load had been lifted off her shoulders. She felt free and wanted to laugh and cry at the same time.

Casper travelled to Bristol and returned after a week. "I found us a house there, and while I was walking around, discovered something else," he told the three women.

Sally couldn't believe that they were living in a fancy house, and the first night that they had arrived in Casper's town house, she had slept for fifteen hours straight on the comfortable bed. For the first time in her life, she had her own bedroom, and it was very pretty. Casper had gone out of his way to make the lives of the three women very comfortable. And what's more, they had two maids who waited on them hand and foot, seeing to their every need. Life had truly changed for the three women.

"You all suffered for so many years and from now on, all that you will see is good days. You shall eat the good of this land for the rest of your lives," he'd told them when they tearfully thanked him.

The clothes he'd bought them were magnificent. Sally was wearing a yellow dress with black flowers, while her aunt and Mrs. Claire wore similar pink gowns with flowers on them. They were like twins, and she was happy at the strong friendship that had developed between them. What made Sally even happier was that Casper was clearly besotted with her aunt, and she was happy that Aunt Anne could finally have a husband who loved her and a family of her own.

"What did you find out?" Claire asked. They were in the small parlour taking tea and hot buttered scones. They were truly living a luxurious life.

"I made friends with a fellow whose services were terminated from the Manor because of some foolish issue which he wouldn't share with me, but he told me that Oliver didn't die. Nine years ago, the boy was accused of pouring

188

hot broth on his father's face. According to the man, Grant Winchester rarely leaves his rooms because he was badly burned."

"Oliver didn't burn Mr. Winchester," Anne said forcefully. "That morning that we left, Mr. Winchester came to the kitchen and ...." she bit her lower lip.

"That man wanted to molest my aunt," Sally said. "Yes, Aunt Anne, I have grown up now and know what happened. But as he grabbed Aunt Anne's dress and tore it, Tubby jumped on him."

"Who is Tubby?" Casper asked.

"He was my cat, and Oliver's. She scratched Mr. Winchester, and he staggered towards the large cauldron that was on the fire. I remember Aunt Anne used to boil bones overnight for stock and broth, and he fell into the cauldron. We ran away then, and we didn't know what happened after that."

"You remember all that?" Anne looked at her niece in surprise. "You were so young."

"Like it was yesterday!"

"Well, as I was saying," Casper continued with his tale. "Apparently Mr. Winchester told everyone that it was Oliver who poured broth on him, and they started chasing him, but he got away. Oliver didn't die."

"What if they caught him and hurt him?" Sally put a hand to her throat. Her Oliver might still be alive, but she didn't want to give herself any false hopes. If he was being pursued years ago, someone might have captured him, and he could be in prison or worse, stoned to death.

"That man said they searched for him for many months but believe that he must have joined the Gypsies some years back. Those Gypsies often travel all over England and even here in London. If Oliver joined up with them, then he could be alive somewhere."

"My son," Claire said, shaking her head. "Why did I trust my sister?"

"Mrs. Claire, this means that there's a chance your son is still alive. The Gypsies are back in Potter's Cove, and we could travel there and find out more. If he is in London, they can lead us to him. If he's still with them, we shall find him."

"How soon can we leave for Potter's Cove?"

"I have already made arrangements, and first thing tomorrow morning, we'll all be on our way. I also happened to find us a good house to live in as we work on getting your property back from your sister. Now that I believe Oliver is still alive, he should come into the inheritance his father left him."

19

RIVERS IN THE DESERT

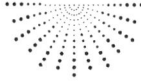

I t was a stroke of great luck that the first Gypsy man Casper asked about Oliver was Manfrid.

"That young man comes and goes. He wants to belong to us, but then again, he doesn't fit in."

"Would you know where he is right now?"

Manfrid shook his head, "He came by a few days ago just to see us, then left again. But he isn't far from this place."

"If he happens to show up again, would you please ask him to come to Corner Street, House Number Seventeen, and ask for Casper Trent?"

Manfrid looked at him suspiciously. "Why do you want to see Oliver? You might be the people who have been hunting the poor boy all these years, as if he were an animal."

Casper shook his head, "I was his father's valet many years ago." He saw the incredulous look on Manfrid's face. Of course, with the way he was well dressed and his polished manners as well as the fancy carriage, no one could mistake him for a valet, not by a long shot. "I said I used to be, but I happened to go to America, where the tide turned for me. Please just ask Oliver to come and find me, and I promise you that he will be safe."

Manfrid pointed a bony finger at him, "Be sure that you treat that young man well, or I will put the curse of the Gypsies on you, and for the rest of your life, you will live like a vagabond."

Casper nearly laughed out loud at how ridiculous the man sounded, but he restrained himself. This man held the key to finding Oliver, if he truly was the person they sought. Casper had a strong feeling that he was on the right path, and he prayed that for Mrs. Claire's sake, they would find her son. He would be her comfort after losing her husband so early.

At the time that Casper was talking to Manfrid about Oliver, the young man was hiding in some bushes very close by. He heard everything the two men were discussing but didn't want to reveal his presence until he was sure that this wasn't a trap. As far as he was concerned, his mother had stopped searching for him years ago, as she had problems of her own, too many to count.

He still slipped into the manor from time to time and visited the dungeon, and he had overheard two servants talking about the misfortunes that had befallen his sister Maeve and his brother. Apparently, Maeve had eloped with some man who took her to Tuscany. Nothing would have been heard of her again, had she not taken her personal maid with her. As it is, once they got to Tuscany and the young maid saw the conditions that Maeve and Kent were forced to live in, she'd run away and returned to England to let his mother know about it. But what conditions those were, Oliver had no idea.

He saw the well-dressed stranger shaking hands with Manfrid, and then get into his carriage and ride off. It was his curiosity that took him to Corner Street to search for house number seventeen, and he walked up furtively, eyes darting here and there just in case it was a trap.

He knocked on the door and then ran back down the steps to wait for it to be opened.

"So, I heard that you have been asking about me." Oliver avidly examined the smartly dressed man who had opened the door and was holding it.

"And who might you be?" The man was looking at him strangely.

"Oliver Winchester."

The man shook his head. "The person I seek is Oliver Burnham, the son of my old master."

"And what is your master's name?" There was something about this man that interested Oliver.

"Mr. Oscar Burnham. He used to live in the large manor with his wife and son."

Oliver frowned. "The only large manor around here is the one owned by Mr. and Mrs. Winchester, my parents. I have never heard of Oscar Burnham." He frowned.

"Are your parents still alive then, and is there a way I can speak with them?"

Oliver raised his shoulders and then dropped them again. "You could try but I don't know if they will be willing to speak with you."

"Why is that?"

"They are very private people."

"Don't you live with them?"

"No, we're estranged, and I live alone now."

"If you don't mind my asking, when and how did you get estranged?" There was a light in the man's eyes, and Oliver thought it was excitement, but he could be mistaken.

"It was about nine years ago." Oliver frowned as he thought about that day that had changed his life. "I woke up because I thought I heard someone screaming. The sound came from the kitchen, and I rushed there."

"Why? You couldn't have been more than six at the time."

"No, I had just celebrated my tenth birthday."

"Go on."

"I thought something might have happened to Sally or her aunt, who was the cook." He once again fell silent.

"Was it any of them?"

"No, it was my father, and he was badly burned."

"Oh no, what happened?"

Oliver shook his head, "I don't know but I noticed that the kitchen door leading to the backyard was wide open, even though it was very early in the morning," He nodded, "Oh yes, I noticed Tubby. She was licking something on the floor close to where my Pa lay."

"Tubby?"

Oliver nodded, "She was my cat, but she died two years ago. She was really old, but I kept her last two kittens."

"What happened to your father? Did he die?"

"No, my father is still alive, though he's been bedridden since then. I don't think there's really anything wrong with his legs, but I think the bad scars on his face and chest make him ashamed to be seen by people. So, he just stays upstairs and only comes out of the house at night, hiding in the shadows."

"I thought you said you were estranged from your father. How did you see him?"

"That I am, but I sneak back to the house."

"Why?"

Oliver opened his mouth to speak then faltered, "Why are you asking me so many questions?"He looked at the stranger suspiciously.

The man laughed briefly, "Forgive me, but I would really like to find my master, and maybe his son. But that man you say is your father isn't him. Would you know if Mr. Burnham sold the estate and manor to your father?"

"I know nothing of the sort because I lived there as a child. It might have happened before I was born," he shrugged, turning as if he would walk away.

"Wait," Casper called out.

"What is it?"

"My name is Casper. Would you like to come in for a minute?"

"No, I have to go and prepare some food for the man in the-" he broke off as if he realised that he'd said too much. "I have to go now."

"Please, just a moment," the man turned and spoke to someone inside the house, anda very beautiful young woman came to the door. There was something familiar about her.

"Oliver?" She called out in a hoarse whisper, her hand going to her throat.

"Sally?" He felt like his feet were rooted to the ground, his eyes never leaving her face.

She gave a joyful laugh and ran down the steps to fling herself into his arms. He caught her just in time and staggered backward a few steps before he steadied himself.

"I never thought I would see you again!" Sally was laughing and crying at the same time. "I came back here three years ago, but I was told that you were dead. Then one day in London I went to the circus and saw someone like you, but the person was wearing Gypsy clothes," Sally knew she was rambling, but she couldn't believe that Oliver, her Oliver, was here in the flesh.

"I'm alive. When did you go to the circus? Because Manfrid took me to London three years ago, and I was helping him put up the tents and carry out necessary repairs. It's true that at the time I had to dress like a Gypsy. Why didn't you call out? I would have come to see you."

Sally didn't want to tell Oliver she had gone to the circus with Edgar. He would ask too many questions which she wasn't really prepared to answer.

"I didn't want to call out just in case it wasn't you and the person was offended. But what happened to you when I came back here three years ago? It was on the same day that Maeve was getting engaged."

He was astonished. "That day I was at the house, but I didn't care for the celebrations. I saw a young woman dart out of the house. She was wearing a blue dress, and something about her troubled me."

"That was me," Sally said excitedly. "I had come to look for you, then when I was told that you had died years ago, I ran to catch the train back to London because I had left Aunt Anne there." Sally linked her arms in his and dragged him to the house. "Come, Aunt Anne and Mrs. Claire are inside."

Oliver allowed himself to be pulled into the house. His throat felt constricted, and he thought he was going to cry. He'd never forgotten Sally and had often wondered if she was still alive. That she had finally come back to him after twelve years was incredible, and he thought he was dreaming.

The moment he stepped over the threshold and into the house, a woman he'd never seen before moaned and held her arms towards him.

"Oliver," she cried out passionately and tenderly and he frowned.

"Do you know me?"

"Yes!" She rose to her feet shakily and walked towards him. "You're the spitting image of your father." She drew closer and cupped his face in her palms. "I never thought I would ever see you again." Tears were coursing down her face. "My son, oh my dearest Oliver."

"What?" He took a step back, pulling away from her.

"You're my son. It's a long story. I haven't seen you since you were a couple of days old."

"Why did you leave me?" he asked angrily, thinking about the suffering he had undergone his whole life.. "If you're my mother, who is the woman living in the manor?"

Claire sighed, "It's a long story, but we need to find out what happened to your father."

"Well, I have to go." As happy as he was to see Sally, he felt overwhelmed with emotions. After all the pain he'd endured, here was this fancily dressed woman who claimed to be his mother. Where had she been when he was suffering? What was it she wanted from him now? "I have to go."

"Please, don't go," Claire begged. This was her son, and she wasn't going to let him out of her sight again. "Oliver, your father is dead, and you're all I've got."

"Where were you when I needed you?" His tone was harsh, and he pushed down the guilt he felt when he saw her flinch like he'd struck her. "All those years, I was tormented by Maeve and Kent, and then my mother, well, the woman at the manor who I thought was my mother, never bothered about me. The only time she cared was when she was whipping me," he lashed out. The anger he carried inside had to come out, and he didn't care that it was directed at this sweet-looking woman. "Why didn't you come and take me away then?"

"Oliver," Sally put a hand on his arm. He was trembling, and he allowed himself to be led to a chair. "Please calm down, and we'll tell you everything."

"This is too much," he moaned, bowing his head and covering his face with his palms.

"Please listen as I tell you what happened to your mother, and then you can decide what you want to do after that." Her soft voice got to him, and he nodded. She told him everything Casper had shared with them, and about Aunt Anne being to the asylum and how they had found Mrs. Burnham there.

"You see, it wasn't your mother's fault that she left you," Sally said softly. "She nearly died because of losing you. When Aunt Anne and I went to live in the asylum, she carried a piece of wood around which she had named Oliver. Your mother never forgot about you. It was just horrible circumstances that led to your being separated from her. Both of you have suffered." Sally touched his cheek. "Look at your mother and the pain she has been through for years. You were snatched out of her arms when you were a newborn. Can you imagine the anguish she's lived with? No wonder she ended up in Bedlam."

Oliver raised his eyes and met those of his mother. She looked so broken and he found himself staggering to his feet and then sank down before her. "My mother," he cried hoarsely as he put his head on her lap.

"My son," she nearly choked on the words and stroked his head. "You were dead but are now alive! I am so grateful to God for this."

They wept for a long while, and nobody said anything. Then Sally remembered something.

"Oliver," she called out when he was finally calm.

"Yes, Sally?"

"Whatever happened to the man who used to live in the dungeon? Did he ever tell you his name?"

"Never. He is still there, and I call him Mr. Cage. Why?"

"All these years, I haven't stopped thinking about him and whether he is alive or not."

"What man is that?" Claire asked.

Casper picked up the questions. "Sally shared with me that when you were children you used to go down to the dungeons to visit with someone. Is he still there?"

Seeing as Sally had already spilled the beans, Oliver saw no reason to continue hiding the matter. "As a matter of fact, I was about to leave here so I could take him food. It's getting harder for me to sneak into the dungeons because I have grown tall. I have to really squeeze through the tunnels and especially the one leading from the old well."

"Wait, we need to know how you have been getting in."

Oliver shrugged. "Through the old well at the back of the house."

Casper looked at Claire, who nodded, "When I first came to live at the manor, my husband, your father, told me that smugglers had used the dungeons as their hideout decades before he was born."

"One day when we were talking, Mr. Cage told me the same thing about smugglers, and I thought he might have been one of them, and they had left him behind or something," Oliver frowned. "It is a terrible place for a man to live all these years.

"Why haven't you ever rescued him then?" Sally asked.

"Because he won't come with me. When I became friends with Mr. Manfrid, the Gypsy, he taught me how to make metal clippers. I even cut Mr. Cage's shackles, but he's never left. It's like he's given up on life. He has nothing more to live for. He once told me that he had lost his whole family, and there was no more hope for him. To me it sounded like he was doing penance for some sin or wrongdoing, but he never shared much."

Casper didn't want to raise anyone's hopes. "Is there any way that we can get Mr. and Mrs. Winchester and their children out of the house? I would like to see your Mr. Cage. He might be one of the servants who lived in the manor years ago, and he may be able to tell us what happened to your father."

"That's easy. Mrs. Winchester went to London to see if she can find a way of getting to Tuscany where Maeve and Kent are. I overheard some of the servants talking a few days ago. They seem to have run into some kind of trouble out there, and I think she is trying to bring them home. And like I told you before, Mr. Winchester hasn't left his room ever since he got burned years ago."

"What about the servants who are there? They must be loyal to their masters."

"That they are, and it is the reason why I still have to hide to take food to Mr. Cage. He said I was the one who poured hot broth on his face, and they have been pursuing me all this time because someone, I think it was my mother-" He cleared his throat, "Mrs. Winchester put out a bounty on my head."

∾

Casper knew that if he had to get to the man in the dungeon and find out who it was, he had to involve the village constables. He also knew that having money and being in an influential position opened doors. Still, he was very careful in the way he approached them. They might be loyal to Mrs. Winchester, who was considered the lady of the town, since she and her husband claimed to own the manor.

Fortunately, he found kindred spirits in the two gentlemen. Both claimed that Mrs. Marie Winchester had done their relatives wrong.

"She is a very wicked woman," Bradford Helms, the older village constable said. "I have been seeking for a way of dealing with her, but everyone seems to be afraid of her, even more so now when she lives with a man who is no better than a bandit. After her husband was injured and she said it was her youngest son who did it, which sounded suspicious to me, she brought in a rough-looking fellow to stay in the house. She claims the man is her cousin, but servants talk, and it is rumoured that the fellow is her lover."

"Will you help me free the man in the dungeon?" Casper asked.

"Yes, but if that bandit is in the house, there could be a nasty confrontation. If we have to rescue the man, only skilled men should make the attempt."

"I have lived in America for twenty years," Casper said. "I've battled rogue Indians, cattle rustlers, and even other Wild West bandits. I don't think this would be any struggle for me at all, but we will ask the women and Oliver to stay back because I don't want anything to happen to them."

"Why don't I send someone to find out exactly who is at home, so we know what we're walking into?" Constable Helms asked, "A spy of some sort who is a nondescript fellow and won't raise any alarms with the servants."

It was agreed that a spy would be sent, and he returned with good news. He confirmed that indeed the mistress of the manor had travelled to London while the master never left his rooms. As for the servants, they would not pose a threat. "Those worthless fellows were so busy brewing and imbibing in moonshine that it will be very easy for us to slip in and out without them being aware of whatever is going on. Call it a case of the cat being away and the mice being free to play," he said in a dry voice, and his companions chuckled.

Oliver refused to stay behind when the raid was being executed, and he was the one who boldly walked up to the front door and knocked.

"What do you want?" A clearly drunk man came to the door. No one knew if he was the butler or an ordinary servant. He reeked of stale moonshine, and Oliver wrinkled his nose.

Casper and the two constables pushed their way in, and Oliver followed them. They had brought two more volunteers who would be the lookout men and alert them of any impending danger. "Mr. Burnham told me of the dungeons years ago when I was his valet," he said. "There was a way through the master's den, and he showed it to me, telling me that if ever danger came to the manor, I was to get out through there and save his family."

Oliver walked through the house that he'd lived in as a tormented and rejected little boy, and he blinked hard so the tears wouldn't fall. This place had been torture for him, and all he wanted was to rescue Mr. Cage and get out before he broke down.

Casper led the way to the den and then tapped the panels on the wall. One of them sounded hollow, and he slid it open. The four of them entered. It was a short walk to where Mr. Cage was. The moment Casper saw the hairy man, he let out a long wail, forgetting where they were.

"Hush," Constable Helms said. "Who is this man?"

"This man is my master, Mr. Oscar Burnham," Casper said. "Sir, you are alive."

Oscar Burnham slowly rose to his feet and swayed. "Casper? Is this really you? Where is my wife?"

"Sir, don't speak," the constable said. "We've come to get you out of this place and set you free."

"Leave me to my doom," he wept bitterly. "I couldn't protect my wife and son. This is my just penance."

"Sir, your wife and son are alive," Casper motioned to Oliver. "This is your son Oliver, the same young man who has been taking care of you all these years."

Father and son stared at each other and then fell into each other's arms and wept.

"We need to hurry up and get you out of here before the undesirable elements return."

❧

It was a tense group that waited at Casper's house for the rescue team to return with the freed prisoner.

"What if they get hurt?" Claire was shaking. "I lost my husband and now can't bear the thought of losing my son just as soon as I have found him," she cried. "Oh God, please be merciful to me and spare my son."

Anne was saying a prayer of her own for Casper. She was in love with the gentleman, and he had told her that he would return and then ask for her hand in marriage. Like Mrs. Claire, Sally was praying for Oliver to return safely.

When they heard a carriage pull up to the front door, the three women rushed to open it. The moment Oliver and Casper stepped out and helped someone down, Claire gave a hoarse cry, and her two companions had to hold her up before she crumpled to the ground.

"Claire?" The bearded man squinted against the bright light. His skin was nearly white, with red blotches, as a result of living underground for so many years and not being exposed to the sun.

"Oscar," she whispered, and slid into a dead faint.

"Quick, let's get Mrs. Burnham inside!" He motioned to the two constables, who helped Anne and Sally carry the unconscious woman into the house. They placed her on a long couch and stood back. Everyone wanted to hear this story to the end, so no one took a step further.

∾

Maeve had not only heard about hell, but she now lived what felt like it. For three years, she had been nothing more than a slave. She was forced to do as the man who claimed to be her husband said. But he wasn't just her husband; he was also the man who pimped her out to other men in the underground world of Tuscany.

She had eloped with Cliff ,and for the first month, he'd acted like the besotted husband while he and Kent undertook various dealings which she now knew to be nefarious. When things went wrong for them, Cliff became ruthless and demanded that they pay him back every single penny he had ever spent on them, and the way to do this was turn Maeve into a soiled dove.

"You put me in this mess," she wept as she looked at her brother. Her body was disease riddled, and she had pustules covering her whole body from the head to the knees. Her flesh was falling off, and she looked grotesque. "If you hadn't gambled father's wealth away, you would never have met Cliff, and then I wouldn't have fallen in love with him," she wailed. "See what he has turned me into?"

Kent bowed his head, weeping silently. When he'd been told that his sister was ill and at death's door, he had taken it lightly and hadn't visited for a while. What he was seeing right now broke his heart.

"I'm sorry," he whispered. "What can I do to make your life better?"

"Kill me," Maeve cried. "End my life so this agony can be over."

20

UNBROKEN BONDS

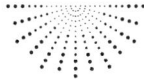

"The day Oliver was born was the best and worst day of my life," Oscar said, holding his wife's hand like he would never let go. Casper had convinced him to have a bath and shave, and the once-handsome man Claire Burnham had loved and never forgotten, emerged. Just as she'd said, Oliver was the spitting image of his father. "I never knew that it would be the beginning of our tribulations for the next twenty-one years." Tears pooled in his eyes. "Had I known the anguish childbirth would have brought you, my love, never would I have put you through such pain."

"But then we wouldn't have had Oliver," Claire said in her soft husky voice. "Even though we have been through so much pain, I believe that we have also been blessed." Her eyes went to Oliver, who hadn't stopped staring at his parents, his real parents. "And see what a fine young man he's turned out to be."

"That's right, "Oscar said, "For years, this child took care of me when I was down in the dungeons. He had no idea that it was his father he was caring for. To him, I was just a stranger in the dungeon, forgotten by everyone. But every single day, he found a way of bringing me water and food." Oscar started shaking, "So many times I wanted to tell him not to return because I was afraid that if Marie knew that he was coming to see me or even knew of my existence, she wouldn't have hesitated to murder him. As he grew, he continued looking so much like me, but I dare not hope that it was my son. It was easier to believe that Marie had killed Oliver than to hope that he was the boy taking care of me."

"It's all my fault," Claire started crying, "If I hadn't begged you to allow Marie and Grant to come and live with us, none of this would have happened. My sister would never have taken over our own home and harmed us like she did."

"My love," Oscar gathered her close. "You should never be sorry for being gentle, kind-hearted, and generous. It's a pity that we were taken advantage, of but none of that was your fault. You were doing your best for your sister and her family."

"Marie caused us so much pain."

"But justice has been served," Oliver said. "Pa, you remember the little girl who used to come down to the dungeon with me?"

"Yes."

"This is Sally," Oliver pointed to /her, "I thought I had lost her when she left."

"I returned to the manor three years ago, on the day that Maeve was getting engaged," Sally pointed out, "But I overheard the servants talking, and one of them mentioned that you had died nearly nine years before."

Casper cleared his throa., "Mr. Burnham, why did these wicked people keep you alive all those years? Why didn't they just kill you and be rid of you?"

Oscar smiled, "Because of my very wise solicitor." Everyone looked at him, and he nodded slowly. "You see, my will as advised by Mr. Blackstone is so ironclad that even I couldn't break it. The moment Claire told me that we were going to have a child, I wrote a will and put a special clause in. That clause stressed that a trust fund was to be set up for the child, whether a boy or girl. But the child couldn't get access to the money until he or she turned twenty-one." Oscar looked at Oliver. "That was the reason they kept you around. Also, there was a clause that if the child didn't make it to the stipulated age of twenty-one, then on the day of that birthday, all the money would revert back to me. If I was dead, the money would go to various charities."

Casper nodded. "So it was in their best interest to keep both of you alive but separated. They made sure you didn't know that your son was alive, and maybe that also saved Oliver's life. But destiny is very powerful, and in the end Oliver found you on his own, even without them. What wickedness."

"Sally and I always wondered why the people who had put you down there never killed you. Now we know."

"Yes, and to keep me barely surviving but not completely lucid, Marie and Grant made sure to feed me once a week. They would bring in that Briggs fellow to scrub me down with lye and water, so I didn't die because of filth. They had it all planned out so they could steal the money I had kept for Oliver."

"Why didn't your solicitor do anything about it all that time? Oliver asked.

"Perhaps I can answer for myself." They all turned to the elderly man who had just walked in. "Mr. Burnham, Mrs. Claire," the old man had tears in his eyes as he stretched his arms towards them. "This is great joy for me. When Constable Helms came by my home to tell me that you had both been found and were alive, I had to get out of bed." He shook their hands. "I have been very ill for many years, and at times I even despaired of my life."

"How did you never ask about us?" Oscar wanted to know.

Titus Blackstone sat down heavily and then leaned forward, "Mrs. Claire had brought her sister to see me just before she gave birth. It was as though your wife had a premonition that something bad might happen to her." Oscar looked at his wife and then back at the solicitor.

"Go on, please."

"They looked happy together and I thought that as sisters they would look out for each other, so when Mrs. Claire asked me to trust Mrs. Winchester, I didn't hesitate. A few months later Mrs. Winchester came to me in deep sorrow. She told me that her sister and brother-in-law, as well as their baby son, had died while on a trip to Paris and were buried abroad. She had documents showing proof of death and burial of the three of you, and I never suspected anything. There was the issue of your wealth. As they were your surviving kin, I saw no trouble in letting them have the inheritance." He stopped talking. "But something odd happened one day. I came by the house and saw Oliver. This was about five years later and what struck me was how much he looked like Mr. Burnham when he was a small boy. You see, I had been Mr. Oscar's father's solicitor and had seen him growing up, so it was easy for me to recognize that this boy was certainly his offspring. For a while I thought he might be a child born out of wedlock, possibly with a maid, but the name of the boy made me very cautious, and I doubted that Mr. Burnham here could have done something so vile as to betray his wife in such a manner."

"What happened then?" Oscar leaned forward.

"The moment Mrs. Winchester realized that I knew about Oliver, she came up with the story that the boy had been brought back to them by a family in Paris. That was another reason I was willing to continue providing them with money. If Oliver was alive, then he would grow up to take over his father's properties. I still believed that Mrs. Winchester had her nephew's best interests at heart." The man's eyes were full of remorse. "I should have dug deeper to find out more, but the Winchesters appeared to be very reputable. What's more, after I had seen Mrs. Burnham with her sister, I believed that they were very close, and that blinded me to the truth."

"Please, don't blame yourself, sir," Oscar said. "Those people fooled everyone, and we never knew how wicked they were."

"I failed you, and your father was my very good friend. I'm really sorry."

"Mr. Blackstone," Oliver broke in. "No one will ever blame you. If anything, you saved my father's life."

"How?"

"By making his will very complicated. If you hadn't asked him to put money in trust for me, they would have killed both of us a long time ago. As it is, they had to keep me around until my twenty-first birthday. But when I ran away, they had to keep Pa alive, hoping they would cash in when my twenty-first birthday came around and the trust fund reverted back to him."

"This family has paid a high price indeed," Casper said. "Mr. Burnham, you were always a good employer, and you saved my life," the young man shook his head. "I owe you my whole life and future."

"We will forever be in your debt," Oscar said, as Claire nodded, "For many years I believed that Claire and Oliver were dead, because that's what Marie told me. "You see, after I had asked you to take my wife and son to London, I didn't expect that Marie would snatch Oliver away."

"We nearly didn't make it out of the house because Mrs. Burnham was very distraught when she couldn't find her son., I dragged her away because I believed you would find Oliver and bring him to London."

"Well, Marie brought him and threatened to kill him if I didn't get rid of Claire. But then bandits rushed into the house. At the time, I had no idea that they were in cahoots with Marie and Grant." No one said a word. "They shot Grant; at least, that's what they made me think," Oscar shook his head. "Then they took Marie to the other room and threatened to defile her unless I told them where Claire was. I lied that she was upstairs still recovering from childbirth. They intended wickedness to my wife so that once she was defiled, I would reject her. Later on, I found out that Marie had planned all this, but it was too late."

Oscar bowed his head and Claire put her hand on his shoulder.

"I was buying time so Casper could get Claire far away. But when they couldn't find Claire, they beat me up, until I was unconscious. When I came to, I found myself down in the dungeon. When Grant and Marie came in to taunt me, that's when I realized they were in on the whole plan with the bandits.

They told me they had caught up with Claire and she was dead, as was Oliver.," His voice dropped, and grief was etched on his face. "I lost all my will to live, and if I hadn't been placed in iron shackles, I would have ended my life." He took his wife's hands and kissed them. "Claire, I would have given up all my wealth in a heartbeat if it would have meant having you and Oliver back."

"Well, with this information now, we can go ahead and arrest those evil people," Mr. Blackstone said. "The constables are just waiting for word from me." He nodded at the two policemen, who nodded back.

"Go ahead," Oscar said, his face as hard as flint, "Let them pay for their wickedness for the rest of their lives."

~

"You will pay what you owe me with the rest of your life," Cliff snarled at Kent. "I'm going to sell you off as a slave and forever you will live like one."

"Why did you turn against us when I thought we were friends?" Kent looked at his sister on the bed. She was barely breathing.

"Friends?" Cliff's tone was mocking. "I wanted the Winchester estate, but imagine my dismay after spending so much money on you and your worthless mother, I find out that it doesn't belong to you."

"That's not true. I'm the heir of my father."

"Yes, the heir of nothing. The manor, which your mother so arrogantly claims, belongs to her brother-in-law. Your mother's stepsister married a man named Oscar Burnham, who was killed years ago. But his son still lives and upon his twenty-first birthday, the boy will show up and claim his inheritance. You lied to me, and I spent all my money on you."

"I didn't know that," Kent turned as white as a sheet. Now he understood why Cliff had made his sister pay with her body, which was now ravaged. "But you didn't have to make my sister suffer like this. Look at her! You have even refused to bring her a doctor, and yet you still expect her to serve the men you lead to this house day in, day out. It's a good thing they are so repulsed by her appearance that they have left her alone."

"And that is the reason I have sold you to become a slave."

Maeve made a sound of distress and the two men looked at her. She raised a feeble hand and beckoned to Cliff.

"What is it, my dearly beloved wife?" he taunted her. "How does it feel to be the Queen of many, as you referred to yourself? And indeed, your worthless body has served many men."

"Please help me," she whispered. He wasn't at all threatened by her because he thought she was too weak and emaciated. He bent over her to poke at her wounds like he normally did when he wanted to cause her pain. At that moment, her hand shot out and he felt a sudden hot and very sharp pain in his chest.

"What?" he felt something gurgling in his throat as he tried to pull back, but the dying woman had gathered all her strength, determined to end her anguish with the death of her tormentor. She twisted and turned her hand, slashing in a downward jerking movement, and then let it fall back on the bed, a satisfied look on her face. Cliff staggered backwards, his guts spilling all over, with blood spurting out of his mouth.

He fell to his knees, dropped his arms, and looked down at his stomach in disbelief. A foul stench worse than had been in the room before filled the air as his entrails poured out of his body. He looked up and saw the sinister smile on his wife's face, her hand still clutching the knife that had disembowelled him.

"Maeve," he whispered, then pitched forward, writhed on the floor, and lay still forever.

"Kent, you're now free. Run, and don't look back."

"Where did you get that knife," he stared at the ugly looking blade in his sister's hand. It was dripping with blood, and all he could see on her face was a satisfied look.

"One of the maids gave it to me when I wanted to slice some peaches. I've kept it with me and have been sharpening it. Now don't ask me any more questions, just leave this place before anyone comes here and finds this worthless fellow's body. Go, Kent, go away."

21
TRUE LOVE WINS

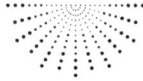

Marie Winchester was in great despair. She'd rushed to London with the hope of finding her son-in-law so he could bail her out of her current predicament. Briggs, the man with whom she had betrayed her husband with for years, the one she thought she had controlled all these years, had turned the tables on her. He was threatening her with dire consequences if she didn't pay him for his silence.

Marie had been waiting so she could force Oscar Burnham to turn over his son's trust fund to her. Oliver was long dead, so she believed, because she couldn't imagine that a small boy of ten could have evaded capture by her men for eleven years. Had he still been alive, she would have forced him to sign over his inheritance, and then he and his father would be dealt with. Briggs hadn't forgiven her for allowing Clifton to marry Maeve. He'd wanted Maeve for himself, but Marie couldn't imagine that her lover would be her daughter's husband. Incensed, Briggs had slowly begun turning the tables on her with his unreasonable demands. He took as mistress one of her own maids, and they blatantly carried on under her roof. The moment she began to protest, he told her he would reveal all the secrets that the Manor had carried for years.

Begging him not to be so hasty, and that she would find a way of making his life better, she had rushed to London to see Cliff. Her daughter's handmaid had told her that Cliff had taken Maeve to Tuscany, and that she was living a terrible life. Marie didn't want to interfere with what she said was the affairs of a man and his wife. Her own interest was in getting money to keep Briggs quiet.

Cliff had refused to meet with her, and it was with a tremblign heart that she returned to Bristol. As soon as she stepped off the train and got to the manor, two constables showed up and handcuffed her. She didn't even put up any kind of resistance, as they took her not to the village police station, but to another beautiful semidetached house on Corner Street. She was shocked to find that Briggs had also been arrested, and he lay on the ground, shackled with fetters of iron. It was all over for them, and it was there in that house that she knew that her sins had finally caught up with her. There was no way out of this. She listened as Oscar accused her before the police constables.

As Oscar's voice faded into silence, Marie saw herself as she really was, something that had never happened before. Her face fell, and she began to sob in earnest. Marie had never loved anyone but herself, not even her children and husband.

From the time she was a little girl, she had learned how to manipulate people. It was always a game with her. When Oscar, the man she desired above anything else because of his wealth and good looks, had married Claire, she had felt that she'd been treated shabbily, deprived of the wealth and love that should have been hers. She had ended up married to a worthless fellow. That was when she had started scheming on how she would make her sister pay. She'd nearly succeeded, but now it had all burned to ashes.

Her eyes dropped to avoid the disdain she could see on everyone's face. The Oliver she thought had died was seated before her, as were her sister and brother-in-law. She even recognized the woman who had been her cook for about three years, and she wondered what she was doing here. Maybe she was another witness against her, but no one would tell her. There were other strangers in the room, but she didn't care about them. These three were the ones she had sought to destroy, but now everything had turned against her. She had no idea if her children were even still alive, and as for Grant, he had his own cross to bear, so she didn't care about him at all.

"Why, Marie?" Claire asked in a soft voice, "I really loved you, and I wanted to help you and your husband. You're my sister, and I wished you well. Why did you tear my family apart and keep me away from my husband and son for all these years? Why?"

"Because you had it all!" Marie screamed, an ugly look on her face. "My father married your mother when you were two years old, and you became his favourite daughter. I was seven and all of a sudden, I lost my father's affection, as he poured it all on you."

"I'm sorry."

"Are you?" Marie demanded, "And if that was not enough, I saw Oscar first and wanted him, but he only had eyes for you."

"But you were already married to Grant when Oscar came to marry me."

"No, I had met him long before, and I thought he was interested in me." She covered her face. "He would come to the house, and I thought he was courting me because you were just fourteen and he was twenty. He waited for you, and I thought that I would make him jealous, so I took up with Grant. I thought that if he saw me with Grant, he would turn to me, but it never happened."

"Marie, I didn't know any of that, and I'm terribly sorry." Claire broke down. She couldn't imagine that the sister she had loved so much and wanted to help had been her worst betrayer. "You would have been happy with Grant if you only let yourself."

"Grant is weak," Marie scoffed, dashing her tears away. "We wanted to have what you had, to live the kind of life you and your husband were living."

"To the extent of murdering your own sister?"

"I used to see Oscar watching me." A sly look came into her eyes, and Sally thought she was looking at the very epitome of evil. This was a woman who had no conscience, even though she broke out into tears from time to time. She was probably pretending to be remorseful, but her eyes told of the wickedness that lived in her heart. "And I knew he desired me."

Claire made a choked sound and shook her head in disbelief. "My dear," Oscar took her hands and held them. "There has never been anyone for me but you. If there was ever a time I looked at Marie, it was to wonder at the evil that festered within her soul. I never wanted them to come and live with us, but you were so distraught when your sister and her family fell into dire straits. That's how much I loved you, enough to put up with this wicked woman and all her evil schemes and manipulations."

"My own sister hated me so much," Claire whispered. "I lost years of my husband's and son's lives ."

"I wanted you to suffer, so when your son was born and you went into depression, I urged Oscar to have you committed, for you were mad. He refused, and I had to force his hand. I believed that if he saw how well I was taking care of Oliver, then he would turn to me. But that would never happen as long as you were still alive."

"So, you hired bandits, led by this fellow." Oscar sneered at Briggs, who was cowering. "You brought them in to defile my wife, and possibly even murder her, but Casper had taken her away. You made your hoodlums beat me up and lock me in the dungeons."

"If I couldn't have you, then no one else could," Marie said.

The police constable gave a harsh laugh. "You will spend the rest of your life inprison, and may God have mercy on your demented soul."

"I don't deserve this, please forgive me," Marie pleaded. "It was Briggs who forced me to do it."

Briggs growled. "She's a liar. She paid me to carry out her plans."

Casper shook his head in disgust. "It is human beings like the two of you who epitomise the worst form of evil in this society. You can be sure that your sins have found you out, and you will pay. For every year of horror that you put this family through, yours will be ten times worse."

"Have mercy, please! I need to find my children. They are suffering. Please spare me so I can find them and bring them back home." She looked at Oliver beseechingly. "Maeve and Kent are your cousins. Have you no mercy for them?"

"To which home?" Oliver asked her at last, facing the woman who had tormented him all his life. "Because of you, I lived among the Gypsies. I slept in the forest, when all this time the manor belonged to my father. Maeve and Kent made my life miserable. Why would I want to show them any mercy?"

"Please," Marie sobbed, the reality of what was to come finally hitting her.

"You made a man live in a dungeon for twenty-one years. It is by the grace of God that he didn't die down there, or we would never have known what happened to the poor man. You treated his heir worse than one would an old dog. This boy started living in the forest when he was ten years old, while your own children celebrated and feasted on what was rightfully his. What kind of heart is within you?" Constable Helms shook his head. "You will be severely punished, both of you, and your husband too."

∽

Three Months Later

There was a double wedding at the manor, whose gates were thrown wide open to let everyone in. The reason for the delay in having the two couples wed was because Claire begged her two companions to wait for the manor to be remodelled. They had been her help and refuge in the asylum, when she'd never expected to leave, and she wanted to do something special for the two of them.

Walls were torn down and rebuilt, but perhaps what made the hearts of especially Sally and Oliver glad was when walls were put up underground to block all the tunnels. Every entrance from anywhere was examined and a strong wall built to seal it. Never again would anyone be held in the dungeons. They would remain forever sealed.

Another reason for the delay was the sudden public interest in the case against Marie and Grant Winchester, as well as their accomplice Briggs. People came from far and wide to listen to the case against the three, and when the sentence was pronounced, Grant Winchester collapsed. Before a doctor could be summoned, he breathed his last. His widow and her lover were each sentenced to hang, but this was changed to life imprisonment. Briggs tried to break out of prison a few days later and was killed by the police constables pursuing him. Marie Winchester would spend five years in prison before she died, broken and alone, with no family or friends. She never found out what had happened to her children, and people thought that it was just punishment for her wickedness. She'd separated a family, and in the end, it was her own that was ripped apart forever.

Now that the wicked people had met their fate and were either dead or in prison, laughter returned to the manor.

For many days, neighbours and friends flocked to see Mr. and Mrs. Burnham and their son, of whom it was said had risen from the dead. They all recalled being told that the couple and their infant son had died in Paris while visiting relatives.

As Sally and Oliver exchanged their vows, Aunt Anne and Uncle Casper were doing the same. Even though Marie and Grant had emptied the family coffers, Oliver's sizeable inheritance held in trust until he had turned twenty-one had matured. Because of the interest that had accrued, there was so much money that Oscar's eyes crossed when his solicitor, the good Mr. Blackstone, told him how much it was.

Oscar was of the opinion that he should sell some of his land so he could use the money to put his estate right. His son wasn't willing that the land should go to an outsider. Oliver had two requests to make to his father with regard to the land. First was that twenty acres be given to the Gypsies as a gift so they would always have a place to stay after their wanderings. They had protected and nurtured him for several years, and he felt that they deserved to have their own land. They would no longer be squatters, judged harshly and discriminated against by other people. The second request Oliver made was that Casper be allowed to purchase another twenty acres so the estate could be rebuilt with the money he paid. Casper made a good offer for the land, and his plan right after he returned from his honeymoon in Paris was to set up a home for him and his beautiful wife, Anne.

~

Anne and Sally made their husbands take them to the old cemetery where the latter's parents were buried. "You never saw their graves," Anne told Sally. "This is one way of putting the past behind us and reaching for the future."

"Do I have to say something to them?"

"No, I just wanted you to know that your parents loved you and would have wanted you to have a wonderful life. They were taken from us when you were so small, and the years since have been filled with so much pain for you, Sally. I want to ask you for your forgiveness for any pain and anguish I may have caused you."

"No, Aunt Anne, you never caused me any anguish or pain. Bad things happened to us, but none of them were your fault."

"Sally," Anne held her niece close even as their husbands stood a short distance away, never uttering a single complaint about the odd request. "You lost your childhood and had to grow up before your time. I should have protected you, but you became the person who cared for me.

You never once showed anger or impatience, even though I know it must have been a very tough time for you."

"Aunt Anne, you took me when I was little and made me your daughter," Sally sniffed. "You could have as well sent me off to an orphanage so you could carry on with your life. Because of me, you never married, even though a number of suitors showed interest. You gave your life for me, so when you needed me, I was there for you."

The two women stood arm in arm looking down at the slabs that had been laid to cover the graves of their beloved. A few moments later, they returned to the Manor where the celebrations were in full swing. Gifts were bestowed to both couples, but they knew that the best ones were that they had found each other and been granted the grace to love and be loved.

The two large cakes were shared with family and neighbours, and everyone would talk of the double wedding for years to come. It was as if a miracle had happened upon the people of Potter's Cove.

~

"I never thought I would see you again." Sally leaned toward her husband when they returned to their bedchamber later that evening. The celebrations were still going on downstairs, but the couple needed to be alone. He had filled a plate with cake, for he knew how much Sally loved it, and coaxed her upstairs to the new bedchamber. Gone were the days when he would have to listen with a pounding heart for the footsteps of his mother or siblings on the way to torment him. From now on, he would only hear sounds of joy and laughter.

"When I look at you, my love, I feel like I'm dreaming," he murmured as he pulled her close. "Twelve long years of not seeing you but hoping and praying that we would one day meet. I was so afraid that some other man would steal you away, and that you would forget all about me."

Sally thought about Edgar Gillen and decided that there would be no secrets between them. They would begin their new life together with open hearts and honesty between them. She decided to tell him everything.

"When I was fifteen, a wealthy man came to the institution. His beloved aunt was committed there, and we met," she looked down. "His aunt died, but he continued coming, and he even asked me to be his wife."

Oliver pulled away. "Did you say yes?" He could not believe how jealous he felt. "Please tell me that you rejected his proposal."

"Oliver, you've got to understand that I was all alone taking care of Aunt Anne and your mother. The institution came under new management, and they raised the fees. Even though I was working there, what I was making wasn't enough to enable us to have private quarters. I was desperate, Oliver." She held out her hands beseechingly, but he ignored them, and she dropped them back on her lap.

Oliver shot to his feet and moved around the room. One part of him didn't want to hear the rest of the story, but he knew that he would never have peace until he knew everything, "So you married him?" He sneered. "Are you a bigamist?"

Sally looked at him long and hard and he felt uncomfortable.

"What happened?" He barked at her, and she flinched.

"Edgar was honourable enough to wait until I turned eighteen before we could get married. But he insisted on an engagement and I agreed, so that he would pay for bed and board for the three of us. When I turned eighteen, Uncle Casper showed up, and my aunt got better," Sally smiled sadly. "Aunt Anne reminded me of the promise I had made just before she fell ill. I must have been about twelve when I told her that my heart would always belong to you, and you were the only man I ever wanted to marry. I told her that when I was fifteen, I had come to the manor and was informed that you had died. Aunt Anne said the only way I could be sure was if I returned to Bristol with her and visited your grave to prove that you were really dead. Uncle Casper came and sorted everything, putting matters right. I told Edgar that I couldn't marry him."

"He must have been angry. "Oliver returned to her side. "I'm sorry."

"Angry is putting it mildly. He was enraged, and he threatened to toss me into the debtor's prison because I owed him money for taking care of me. Thankfully, Uncle Casper stepped in and paid him off, with interest. I was happy to leave London because I saw another side of Edgar that I had never imagined existed." She trembled, and he held her. "He really scared me."

"You're safe now, and no one can ever harm you."

"So, you forgive me?" she looked up, uncertainty in her eyes.

"My darling, you had to do what you did to keep my mother and Aunt Anne alive and safe. Sally, you humble me, and I don't know how I'll ever repay you. I'm sorry, my love." She placed a finger on his lips, realizing that she had to reassure him of her love. "Don't apologise, because you have nothing to be sorry about."

He kissed her palm. "I couldn't bear the thought of you loving another man, and I behaved badly. I love you deeply, and having you back in my life is like getting a new lease on life."

"You stole my heart when I was only six, and you have held it ever since. Edgar was just a means to an end. Oliver, I love you so much, and forever my heart belongs to you."

He pulled her close and held her tight, seeking her lips and putting an end to further conversation.

~

Anne held Casper's hand as they stood on the porch outside, listening to the joyous sounds inside the house. So much good had happened to her in such a short time that she thought she was dreaming.

"Make sure that your thoughts are only good ones." Casper drew her closer. "I don't ever want you to remember your years of pain." He traced the line of her jaw with his finger, then pulled her closer for a long kiss. "When I was in America, I used to look up at the stars and wonder if I would ever see England again. I left here in shame and humiliation but returned as a victor."

"Did you ever get tempted to marry someone while you were there?"

"Many times," he said. "And Old Mr. Stone even tried to encourage me to do so, but something always held me back." He looked down into her face. "It was you all the time, my darling. I knew that if I married a woman in America, I would never leave."

"I'm glad you waited for me, just as I waited for you," she said. "When my first husband died, I believed that I would be alone forever because I had loved him so much. Then Sally's parents died, and I had to take her into my life. She was all I wanted, and bringing her up gave me so much joy, as well as a purpose. But you came into my life and now have enriched it so much more."

"You humble me with your love, Anne."

"That goes both ways, and you are the best part of the rest of my life."

Casper knew exactly what his new wife meant, because that was also how he felt about her.

EPILOGUE

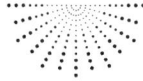

"**W**hat do you think happened to your cousins, Maeve and Kent?" Sally slipped her small hand into her husband's large calloused one. "Do you think they will ever come back here?"

Oliver stopped and turned to his wife. It was early spring, and they were taking a walk around the well-manicured lawn. Sally was due to give birth any moment now, but she had refused to sit still. Everyone fussed over her and she couldn't be happier, but the moments she spent with her husband were precious to her. This baby would be here soon enough, and then she would take on the role of being a mother, but being a wife and friend to Oliver was so important that she didn't want to waste a single moment of it.

"My love, I don't want you to even think about unpleasant matters."

"Oliver, I know that Kent and Maeve really made you suffer. It used to make me so angry when I saw how badly they were mistreating you. Many times, I wished I was big enough so I could bang their heads together and make them stop being so mean." She looked deep into his eyes. "But it is time to forgive and let go of the past. That is the only way we will be able to live a truly abundant life."

Oliver brushed his wife's cheek, "I have forgiven and, as you say, will let go. Once in a while the past may come up and the bitterness may threaten to rise again. But I have you to remind me of the grace that we have received. My parents have also forgiven Aunt Marie and Uncle Grant. We don't ever want to have that dark cloud hanging over our heads."

"I'm so happy to hear that. Mrs. Winchester is in prison for life, and her husband is dead. But what if Maeve and Kent return? Will you make room for them here?"

"That is all in the past now, and I doubt that they will want to show their faces around here again, not after what they did. But enough of that," he said as he dropped a swift kiss on her lips. "My family has been restored and soon," he placed a large hand on her abdomen and the baby kicked, causing them both to laugh, "another generation of my family will be born. This child, and those to follow, will only see goodness and none of the pain we had to go through.

"May the Lord allow it to be so," Sally whispered, placing her hand over her husband's, which was still on her swollen abdomen.

Then she felt something like a sharp pain in her lower abdomen and winced.

"What is it my love?"

"It's time," she whispered.

∽

As a baby boy was being born to Oliver and Sally, hundreds of miles away in the small mining town of Tarquinii in Tuscany, a woman was taking her last breath. Kent had stolen out of Cliff's house with his sister, carrying her as one would a baby, after wrapping her in thick blankets. They were foreigners in this land, and them being found in a room with Cliff's dead body would have serious repercussions for them.

Kent knew for a fact that the house that Cliff had boasted of as his property belonged to one of the Madams he worked for as a pimp. He knew that it wouldn't be long before the mutilated body was discovered, and he wanted to be as far away from that ugly scene as possible. The only way to escape was to hide in the mining town and wait for a suitable moment to return to England.

Maeve's breathing was quite laboured. "Kent, I told you to run away, not to take me with you. I'll only hamper your progress, and since my life is over, I just want you to go on with yours."

"Maeve, please don't do this to me," Kent Winchester pleaded with his sister. "I promise to take you back home. Just hold on for a few days while I work in the mines to get some money for our fare back to England. I know our mother will be happy to see us."

"Home?" she whispered, her skin turning pale as life slowly ebbed out of her. She motioned for him to help her sit up, and he did so. "We have no home, Kent." she said with deep regret. "You heard what Cliff said, that our parents stole the estate from our mother's sister. We have nowhere we can call home, at least I don't. But you can go back and make something of yourself, Kent. Do good, and you will reap wonderful rewards. I couldn't let Cliff destroy your life like he did mine. One of us should live to tell the story."

"We can both do it. See, you're getting better now, and even sitting up."

"Kent, we need to beg for forgiveness."

"What?"

"Oliver. Find him and tell him I'm sorry. He said that we would one day pay for our evil deeds, and that day has come. You can go back home and beg him for forgiveness, and once he sets you free, live on and be good. Name your first daughter after me, and teach her that evil never pays."

"You can tell him that yourself, Maeve. Please get better, and then we can go home."

"I'm tired," she said. "Help me lie down again." Kent didn't care that as he touched his sister, her flesh continued to fall off her disease-ravaged body. All he could see was the love he had for her, but how he'd twisted it and landed her into this horror that she was now in. "Promise me that you will find Oliver."

"We'll do it together," he said stubbornly. "I want you to sleep and then I will go and find

some oatmeal, so you can regain your strength. Your body will heal, and you'll be whole again. Don't give up."

She gave him a sad smile and shook her head. "Kent, I forgive you for all this. Be at peace as I go," and she closed her eyes forever.

Kent stumbled out of the shack in the darkness, tears coursing down his face. This was what someone, he couldn't remember who, had once told him.

"The wages of sin is death," but at the time he and his family had been living large on the wealth of someone else. Shame

and remorse filled his heart as he thought about how he and Maeve had tormented Oliver. They had denied him food, and many times Kent tried to strangle him to death while he slept, but that ferocious cat always rescued him.

Because of his follies, Maeve was dead, and he, who had once been the talk of the town for his looks and family's wealth, was now nothing more than a scavenger. Clifton had used him, but he had brought this upon himself. He didn't know if he would ever see his parents again, because here he was in hiding. If the authorities found Cliff's body, he would be the first suspect because the servants in that house had seen how emaciated Maeve had been for weeks. No one would believe that such a weak woman would have dealt a fatal blow to a strong and healthy man. Everyone would say it was him, and he would be locked up in a prison in a foreign country. No one would ever hear of him again.

He needed to return to England and find his parents and beg them to restore Oliver's wealth back to him, if they could even find him.

He wasn't paying attention to where he was going and suddenly the ground gave way. Kent's broken and lifeless body was found at the bottom of a cliff, and since no one knew who he was, he was buried in an unmarked grave a long way from home. Maeve's rotting body was also discovered in the shack and, like her brother, she was buried in an unmarked grave.

～

Everyone in the room was silent, watching as the beaming grandmother and greataunt swept in majestically, the former holding their bundle of joy.

"It's a boy, and how like you he is, Oliver." Claire held out her grandson so his father could hold him. "Behold, I present to you Oscar Oliver Burnham the Third."

Oliver smiled down at his sleeping son and then looked back up at his mother. His desire was to see the woman who held his heart and make sure that she was all right. He would play with his son later. Right now, Sally was his first priority.

"Ma, how is Sally?"

"Tired but elated. She is a strong woman, and she has done us proud."

"May I go and see her now?"

Everyone laughed, but it was his father who answered.

"Go ahead son. Go and make sure that your wife is all right. This baby is going nowhere, and from what I can see, his grandmothers won't be handing him over to anyone else soon."

Oliver rushed into the bed chamber, eyeing the midwife who bared her teeth at him. He ignored her hissing sounds, all eyes on his wife.

"My darling!" He drew closer to the bed.

"Have you seen him?"

"Yes. Ma says he looks like me." He kissed her forehead. "But I wanted to see you. How are you feeling?"

"Tired but happy." She reached up her hand and stroked his cheek. "Congratulations, Papa."

"You've done well, my Sally." Oliver captured the hand that was stroking his cheek and kissed her palm. "You've brought me so much joy. Who knew when we met as little children that we would end up here, deeply in love and married, with a son of our own." Oliver shook his head in wonderment. "This is a wonder, I tell you. We lost each other for years and then we were granted grace and are now together for the rest of our lives. What more can I ask for, apart from more love so I can bestow it upon you?"

"I have always loved you, Oliver. From the moment I saw you, there was no one else for me."

"I love you, Sally. Thank you for believing in me,even when I couldn't be with you. Thank you for waiting for me."

As he kissed her lips, he could hear their excited family celebrating their baby. Even as Sally slept and he watched over her, Oliver felt deep peace within. This woman was the keeper of his heart, and all was right in his world.

❧

THANK YOU FOR CHOOSING A PUREREAD BOOK!

We hope you enjoyed the story, and as a way to thank you for choosing PureRead we'd like to send you this free book, and other fun reader rewards…

Click here for your free copy of Whitechapel Waif
PureRead.com/victorian

Thanks again for reading.
See you soon!

OUR GIFT TO YOU

AS A WAY TO SAY THANK YOU WE WOULD LOVE TO SEND YOU THIS BEAUTIFUL STORY FREE OF CHARGE.

Our Reader List is 100% FREE

Click here for your free copy of Whitechapel Waif

PureRead.com/victorian

At PureRead we publish books you can trust. Great tales without smut or swearing, but with all of the mystery and romance you expect from a great story.

Be the first to know when we release new books, take part in our fun competitions, and get surprise free books in your inbox by signing up to our Reader list.

As a thank you you'll receive an exclusive copy of Whitechapel Waif - a beautiful book available only to our subscribers...

Click here for your free copy of Whitechapel Waif

PureRead.com/victorian

Printed in Great Britain
by Amazon